CELG

MAY -- 2018

GRAND DESIGNS

Interior decorator Carrie Fraser cannot believe her luck when she is invited to work at beautiful Oakenbury Hall. Nor can she quite get over the owner of the Hall, the gorgeous and wealthy Morgan Harrington. Morgan is bound by his late father's wishes to keep Oakenbury within the family and have children; and the more time Carrie spends with him, the more she yearns to be the woman to fulfil this wish. But the likes of Carrie Fraser could never be enough for a high-flying businessman like Morgan . . . could she?

LINDA MITCHELMORE

GRAND
DESIGNS

Complete and Unabridged

LINFORD
Leicester

First published in Great Britain in 2013 by
Choc Lit Limited
Surrey

First Linford Edition
published 2018
by arrangement with
Choc Lit Limited
Surrey

A catalogue record for this book is available
from the British Library.

ISBN 978–1–4448–3687–5

Published by
F. A. Thorpe (Publishing)
Anstey, Leicestershire

Set by Words & Graphics Ltd.
Anstey, Leicestershire
Printed and bound in Great Britain by
T. J. International Ltd., Padstow, Cornwall

This book is printed on acid-free paper

This one's for my cousin,
David Haas, and his daughters,
Susan and Sharon, with my love.

And in memory of my 'butterfly'
brother, Keith, whose wings never
opened so he didn't get his
moment in the sun.

Acknowledgements

The Choc Lit Team and my fellow Chocliteers are second to none for support and encouragement — thank you one and all.

My brother, Eric, and his wife, Sheila, prise me from my work-in-progress from time to time for long walks and even longer lunches, and remind me that there is life beyond the keyboard — thanks, you two.

Thanks to my son, James, for loaning me his name for this book . . . you're the best.

My daughter, Sarah, is my ears at every social event I go to, and I couldn't do it without her — thank you, my darling.

And a big thank you to the Exeter Chapter of the Romantic Novelists' Association — life wouldn't be the same without our monthly lunches.

And keeping the home fires burning, the larder stocked, and the linen bin empty, is my husband, Roger — thank you so much for everything.

1

'Oh, my God! I'm going to be late! Please, please, James, keep going.'

Carrie knew it was ridiculous to give her car a name. All the way from Farchester her ancient Volkswagen Polo had coughed and spluttered, and she was sure it was only her cajoling words that had stopped it juddering to a complete halt.

The map — with the location of Oakenbury Hall ringed in bright pink felt-tip — was open at the right page on the seat beside her, and Carrie gave it a quick glance.

'Come on, James, you can do it. If you get me there in one piece I won't even think about selling you. Promise.'

An easy promise to keep, Carrie giggled to herself, because she couldn't afford a new car anyway. So far, her commissions had been small — a sitting room here, a child's bedroom there. A couple of dining rooms, and a summer house. And now — thanks to her friend, Genifer Bonnet, who was the owner's PA — Oakenbury Hall.

Now what was it Genifer had told her about the owner of Oakenbury Hall? Morgan Harrington. Thirty-six. Unmarried, although he'd been engaged once, and the untangling of the engagement had been acrimonious; that much Genifer had told her although not the exact details.

'Oh, James, I love you,' Carrie said. She kissed her fingers and touched the dashboard. 'Oakenbury Hall at last. Oh, my God, James — it's huge!'

Carrie changed down a gear, and steered her car through the open gates. Rather large and imposing gates, she had to say. They could do with a lick of paint too, but outside work wasn't in her job brief. Still, it would be a shame to have a wonderful interior and yet have the outside looking so unloved. Maybe she'd suggest that at least the gates be painted. Goodness, gaining this commission was so important to her — professionally, financially, and most of all for her self-esteem. She just had to get it.

She drove on up the drive, gazing at the house.

'I think, James,' she whispered, 'I might be falling in love, if it's possible to fall in love with a house.'

A short central flight of steps led to a wide front door. There were three windows on either side, and another two floors above. The stone — the colour of runny honey — glowed. It was as though the house was inviting her in.

Putting on her bravest, most dazzling smile, she ran up the steps to the front porch. But before Carrie could ring the bell, the door was yanked open.

And standing before her was the most delicious man she had ever seen. Tall — a good foot taller than she was — with thick fair hair bleached by the sun, and with a tan that made his smooth skin glow with health. Green eyes with amber flecks in them regarded her with . . . what? Disbelief? Amusement? Pity? It was hard to read his expression. But he seemed to go with the house somehow — each complementing the other. Oh my God — why hadn't Genifer told her the owner of Oakenbury Hall was this gorgeous?

Not that she was looking. Not after Aaron had left her, almost literally, at the altar.

'Mr Harrington?'

'Morgan. You're late.' He lifted his wrist nearer his eyes to check the time on his dazzlingly large watch, and Carrie was given the full benefit of his tanned, muscular forearm, where he'd rolled his blue and white shirtsleeves up above his elbows.

'I know. I'm sorry Mr Morgan. It's just my that car . . . was traffic, the . . . '

'Morgan is my Christian name. And you're talking gobbledygook.'

Oh I know, Carrie thought, I know. She wanted the ground to open up and swallow her whole. She wasn't usually at a loss for words — ones that ran coherently together anyway. Perhaps it was the surprise of such a wonderful house and now this handsome, if rather irritated, man.

'Er, let me take that,' he said, reaching towards Carrie for the things she was carrying. 'We'll dump it over here for the moment.'

Morgan Harrington smiled broadly then at Carrie, showing a perfect set of sparklingly white teeth, but that smile only stiffened Carrie's resolve that she was not going to fall for his handsome face as she had fallen for Aaron's — the rat. Inside he might be pure poison as Aaron had been.

But when his hands touched her arms as she slid her things towards him, Carrie almost stopped breathing with the shock of what that touch did to her. Static electricity: that was all it was, she told herself — she got much the same getting out of her car sometimes.

'Do come in,' he said.

Carrie stepped inside the hall. It was dark and dimly lit, and while she had imagined it might have smelled of beeswax or lavender, or that there might even have been a dog snoozing by the huge grate, there was nothing but an air of tiredness and sadness. And it was dry . . . as though there had been no life in the place for a long time.

'A modern candelabra would be perfect instead of those small wall lights,' Carrie said. 'Coloured glass maybe. You can get really lovely-looking ones in department stores, quite cheaply.'

Oh God, no, she thought — I've got a case of verbal diarrhoea now! As if this man would do cheap!

'Really?'

He raised an eyebrow and Carrie thought she saw the beginnings of a smile twitch at the corner of his mouth. Please, please, don't smile at me, she thought, because she knew it would be a devastating smile and her knees would become more jelly-like than they already were.

'Really,' she said.

'Good to know you have your finger on the pulse,' Morgan said. 'Keen to get on.'

'Making up for being late,' Carrie said, struggling to sound like a grown-up professional and not a hormone-filled fourteen-year-old. 'It's not how I normally do things.'

'Good, good,' Morgan said. He extended a hand towards Carrie. 'Now we've dealt with that lot, we can do the handshake thing.'

'Carrie Fraser,' she said, as she placed her hand carefully in his.

'I rather guessed you were,' he said, the expression on his face telling her nothing. But his eyes — oh his eyes — were telling her something totally different because they were dancing with amusement. He was laughing at her, wasn't he? He could see he had reduced her to mush, and with looks like his that was probably par for the course from women.

Morgan clasped his hand around

Carrie's fingers. His handshake was firm and dry and went on for longer than Carrie had expected. And he hadn't let go yet.

And there was that tingly feeling again. Only stronger. It reminded her of the time she'd touched an electric fence on a walk in the country with her father. It was all she could do not to yank her hand away from Morgan's.

But as politely as she could, she disentangled her fingers from his, taking control of the situation.

'Drawing room,' Morgan said, pushing open a large, heavy door that squeaked on its hinges.

'Um,' Carrie said. 'This, um . . . interesting.'

Dark green wallpaper, patterned with ivy trails, had faded in places where the sun had got to it. The doors were such a dark wood they were almost black. In her mind's eye, Carrie could see the doors stripped to show the beauty of the grain in the wood. Two couches — non-matching — and three differently styled chairs were dotted about the large room as though no one had cared where they were placed.

How could she tell him it was tatty beyond belief? She guessed that Morgan had become accustomed to it over the years and viewed it as normal. He'd probably been used to this room all his life. And his father and grandfather before him if the style of the wallpaper was anything to go by.

'Ghastly, isn't it?' Morgan said.

He laughed then — a huge, rolling, chocolatey sort of laugh.

'I didn't mean to be rude, Mr Harrington.'

'You weren't. I know it's horrible. But call me Morgan. Please.'

'Oh, I don't think so, Mr Harrington. I mean, if we're to keep this on a professional footing . . . '

'You were thinking of some other footing, Carrie?'

Again that flicker of amusement in his eyes.

And again, Carrie got that wishing-the-ground-would-swallow-her-up feeling.

'You look,' Morgan said, 'as though you could do with a cup of coffee.'

Yes, some hot, strong, coffee was just what she needed to bring her to her senses.

'Thank you,' Carrie said, pleased to see the man had the manners to offer her a drink after driving all this way to see his house. 'A cup of coffee would be lovely. Black. No sugar.'

★   ★   ★

'Wow,' Carrie said, as Morgan threw wide the door to the master bedroom. 'This is bigger than I expected.'

And a lot brighter than the drawing room, thank goodness. There were unpainted, wooden shutters at the window, folded back so that light streamed into the room. The oak flooring was polished to a high sheen, either by the application of many feet walking on it over the years, or regular polish. A large Persian rug covered about a third of the floor area — faded in places to a pleasing softness of tone. Oh yes, Carrie could do something with this room.

'If you're out of your depth with it, best say now,' Morgan said.

'I'm *not* out of my depth, Mr Harrington.' Carrie looked up at him, her eyes meeting his, meeting his challenge. The coffee she'd drunk had done its work. She was back in control now and she would need to know his plans for the room.

'Morgan, please,' he said.

'I prefer Mr Harrington — it keeps things more business-like. Do you have any colour preferences for this room?'

'Nothing too girlie — too pink.' He strode across to the bed and ran a hand across the faded paisley-patterned eiderdown. Then he patted it and little swirls of dust rose up into the air.

He was standing, deathly still, staring into space, and Carrie was alarmed. Something bad had happened to this man, hadn't it? She knew it. She'd stood staring into nothingness herself many a time after her father's death, and then Aaron's betrayal.

'Mr Harrington? Are you all right?'

She came to stand beside him. She reached out and laid a hand on top of his, just for the briefest of seconds — a touch she hoped conveyed concern, understanding.

'Yes, fine. I was thinking about something.'

'About this room? The colours?'

'No, not specifically.' His voice held more than a snap of irritation that she'd asked after his wellbeing. 'You'd have carte blanche. I've never slept in this room and I doubt I ever will.'

'Oh,' Carrie said. 'So, you won't be stopping here?'

She waved her arms around the room and the professional in her saw how it would look transformed by colour and with lights in the right places and with flowers on the dressing table. So many grand houses — well, the National

Trust houses she'd been in anyway — had high ceilings, but the ceilings she'd seen so far in Oakenbury Hall were much lower, giving the place a more intimate, homely feel, despite the size of the house itself.

'I haven't decided what to do with the Hall yet. But Cannes is my home now.'

'Oh, but a house like this should . . . '

'Should what?' Morgan Harrington asked, raising one quizzical eyebrow, as though he'd second-guessed what she was going to say, perhaps.

The truth then.

'I was going to say that a house like this should have children in it. But I'm out of order. I apologise. Telling you what to do with your life isn't in my brief.'

'No, it's not,' Morgan said. 'But just out of interest, how many children do you think should be running around here?'

'Three? Four?' She was looking down at her feet as she spoke. 'Look, I'm sorry — forget I said all that.' She looked up and met Morgan's eye. 'Please?'

Morgan marched towards the door.

'We'll continue with the tour, shall we?' he said, his voice not as firm and as authoritative as it had been, and Carrie wondered what raw nerve she'd hit.

Me and my big mouth, Carrie thought as she hurried along the landing behind Morgan, trying to keep up with his long strides. Well, for the rest of the tour of the house she was going to be in professional mode.

* * *

'So, that's it,' Morgan said when they were back in the drawing room.

Carrie waited for him to tell her which rooms she was going to be doing apart from this one and the master bedroom. All of them needed work, in her opinion, although she would only offer it to Morgan Harrington if asked.

Some of the bedrooms had little in them save a double or single bed, a dressing table, wardrobe, and chair. How they cried out for a picture or two — something floral and blousy, perhaps — on the walls. Or some large mirrors to bring reflected light into the darker rooms.

While she waited, she glanced at a newspaper resting on top of a waste-paper basket. The headline leapt out at her.

'Love at first sight. Research proves it is possible. The first five minutes of any relationship can — and often do — seal the deal!'

And then there were pictures of celebrities who had fallen in love at first sight. But across it someone had scrawled *'Rot!'*. Morgan probably.

Carrie smiled to herself. She'd fallen in love with Oakenbury Hall the second she'd seen it, hadn't she? But Morgan Harrington? As handsome as he was? Hmm, best forget about falling in love with him, Carrie, she told herself firmly.

She'd do the job and then Morgan could get back to Cannes, doing whatever he wished with Oakenbury Hall, and Carrie could get back to her life too.

'When would you like my estimate by?' she asked.

'No need,' Morgan said. 'We could shake on the deal.'

He held his hand out towards Carrie and she had no option but to place hers in it.

'Done,' she said, as he squeezed her hand firmly.

She waited for the tingle but it didn't come this time.

'Not quite. Come out for dinner with me tonight and we'll talk some more.'

'Dinner? I don't think so. Now excuse me, I have to go.'

Morgan let go of her hand and for some strange reason Carrie felt as though she had been cast adrift in unknown waters. She reached for her bag on the floor beside the couch, but it slipped from her grasp and the contents shot all over the place.

'Here, let me help,' Morgan said, a huge grin on his face.

Gosh, but he was devastatingly handsome when he smiled.

'No, no, I'll do it,' Carrie said. There were all sorts of personal things scattered about for goodness' sake! She bent down and began to scoop everything back into her bag with her hands, using them like shovels.

'So, that's no to my supper invitation, is it?' Morgan asked, still smiling as Carrie struggled to close the clasp on her badly-filled bag.

'It is, I'm afraid. I don't think it's ever a good idea to mix pleasure with business.'

'And if I think differently?'

'I wouldn't presume to tell you what to think, Mr Harrington. Ever.'

And then, without giving Morgan the time to insist, yet again, that she call him Morgan, or on helping her to the car with her bags, Carrie hurried towards the door.

2

Midnight, and Carrie snapped shut her file . . . she so wanted to ring Morgan Harrington and give him her estimate — even though he'd insisted he didn't want one — before she went to buy paint and wallpaper in the morning, but it was late. It certainly wasn't professional to ring clients at that late hour, but the line between Morgan the man and Morgan the client was becoming distinctly hazy for Carrie now she was home with time to think. She'd tried to be sensible and analyse how she felt but it was no good — she liked the man, and liked him very much, and that was it.

A cold shower, my girl, is what you need, Carrie told herself. The likes of Morgan Harrington are not for you with a fledgling business to run and a sick mother to care for.

Carrie shuddered at the memory of Aaron calling her mother, Louise, 'baggage'. Well, no one was going to call her mother 'baggage' ever again, and she certainly wasn't going to give Morgan Harrington the chance to do so.

Fresh from her shower — warm because she'd chickened out of having a cold one — and wrapped in a ruby-coloured fleece robe, Carrie was padding across the landing to her bedroom when her mobile beeped. She pressed answer.

'Hi Carrie, it's Morgan here.'

Well, so much for her thinking past midnight was too late to make business calls! Morgan Harrington obviously thought otherwise!

'Hi. What do you want, Mr Harrington?'

'Morgan, please.'

'Morgan then,' Carrie said with a sigh — it was going to be easier to give in to him on this issue rather than have him correct her every time she said Mr

19

Harrington. 'I was just thinking of you, actually.'

Oh God, what a crass thing to say!

'Were you?'

'Professionally,' Carrie said.

'Of course. So, what was it you were thinking — er, um, professionally?'

Carrie could hear the smile in his voice — he was flirting with her! And it was oh-so-tempting to flirt back — easier over the telephone than face-to-face.

'That I should let you know I've made a mood board for the master bedroom. The master bedroom is the most important room in any home.'

'Is that a personal or a professional opinion, Carrie?'

'Both.'

'So, tell me what plans you have.'

'Number one: it has to be essentially feminine. All bedrooms should have an element of romance in them.'

'I couldn't agree more. And number two?'

'Um, um,' Carrie began, fully aware

she didn't have a plan number two. With her free hand, Carrie was sketching Morgan on the notepad she always kept beside her bed. Even from memory she was sure she'd caught his likeness pretty well — his high forehead, the way his hair flopped over it so deliciously, hiding his eyes from time to time so that she hadn't been sure if he was looking at her or not.

'Um, tomorrow I plan to buy the paint and source the wallpaper. Then I'm ready to start the day after tomorrow.'

'Ah, that's what I'm ringing about. How will you pay for whatever it is you choose?'

'My credit cards of course. I'll show you all the receipts.'

Honestly! Did the man think she was totally disorganised, just because she'd been a teensy bit late, and had dropped her bag?

'I have your credit card wallet in my hand, Carrie. It had slid partway under the couch.'

'Oh. Right. Well, I'll come and fetch it first thing in the morning then.'

'No need. I'll meet you wherever it is you're going to buy paint and so on.'

'Oh, but you don't have to.'

'I know. But I *want* to. I'd *like* to.'

'You would?'

'Yes, very much. Now what time, and where?'

Talking to Morgan was making her mouth dry so Carrie reached for her glass of water on the bedside table, but she over-reached and knocked her clock onto the floor. Somehow the alarm was activated and the noise echoed in her sparsely furnished room.

'What the hell was that?' Morgan asked, when Carrie at last found the off switch. 'Are you all right?'

'I'm fine. I knocked something over, that's all.'

Carrie sighed — Morgan was going to think she was an incompetent bumbling fool, dropping things, knocking things over.

'Perhaps I could pick you up in the

morning and take you to wherever it is you need to go. I couldn't help noticing your car was a bit reluctant to start.'

'James will get me to Greenbase, no problem,' Carrie said.

'James?' Morgan said.

Was that a hint of jealousy in his voice? Carrie wasn't in the habit of playing games with people's emotions, but it might help keep their new relationship on a professional basis if Morgan were to think there was a man in her life.

'Yes, James. We go back a long way, James and I.'

'Right,' Morgan said. 'Obviously this wasn't a good time to call. I'll have your card at Greenbase for you. What time?'

'8 a.m.'

'8 a.m. it is then. Goodnight, Carrie.'

And then the phone went dead in Carrie's ear. Goodness, Morgan's moods could change quicker than the weather in April, couldn't they? It would be cruel, and rather childish of her to let him think James was her boyfriend for too long. Tomorrow she'd tell him if he mentioned the name.

But only if.

★　★　★

'I'll take it all with me,' Carrie told the assistant in Greenbase.

'Righto. Won't be long. Ten minutes or so.'

Carrie checked her watch, and looked towards the automatic doors. No Morgan yet. She picked up her pen, leaned on the desk, and began doodling on the edge of the paint chart. As if by some magic process it was Morgan's profile that materialised — his noble nose, and the strong set of his chin.

'Not bad. Anyone I know?'

'Oh my God!' Carrie jumped, knocking into Morgan in her surprise, so that he reached for her elbows to steady her. The touch of his hands, even through her jacket, felt as though an electric charge — like jump leads — had shot through her. Her pencil flew from her

24

hand to the floor, and she slapped her fingers over her doodle.

'Too late. I've already seen it.'

Morgan tried to pull the paint chart from under Carrie's hand.

'It's just a doodle,' Carrie said, pressing hard down on the paper.

'A doodle? More of a sketch, I'd say. A sketch which looks uncannily like me?'

Carrie shrugged. How could she deny it? She was a good artist and had won a place at Central St. Martin's to study fine art. But then her father had died and her mother had gone totally to pieces and she'd given up her place. And then she'd met Aaron — and, well, Carrie wasn't going to give *him* any more brain space!

'Don't tell me — you've drawn a love-heart and put our initials either side of the arrow as well?' Morgan tipped his head to one side and looked quizzically at her, a hint of a smile lighting his eyes.

'Don't delude yourself,' Carrie said.

But then Morgan's smile instantly vanished. Carrie thought he looked as though she'd slapped him, and she knew he still had the power to take the commission away from her. 'Sorry. I didn't mean to snap. I'm not at my best first thing in the morning.'

'Then that makes two of us,' Morgan said. 'But for you I made an exception.'

He reached inside his jacket pocket — cream linen, Carrie noted; she had just the same shade in mind for curtains in the breakfast room should Morgan ever ask her to redecorate that — and pulled out her credit card wallet.

'Thank you. I'll make sure I don't put you to any inconvenience again.'

Carrie took the wallet, making sure their fingers didn't touch.

'If you'd accepted my supper invitation then you might have noticed you'd left it behind earlier.'

'I know,' Carrie said. Morgan was making her feel like a naughty child and a little flush of anger burned her cheeks. 'But I wasn't dressed for going out for dinner.'

'It was only to the local pub, Carrie.' Morgan's eyes were burning into hers, and she could see her reflection in them. 'Oh, and by the way, you blush very prettily.'

'*That*, I have to tell you, is not a very original line. And I am *not* blushing! I've got lots to do. I was up until past midnight, as well you know, and I was up very early this morning, and . . . '

'And James got you here on time obviously?'

Morgan looked around the show-room as though searching for someone.

'Of course.'

'But he's not here now?'

Carrie did a mock search with her hand held to her forehead.

'Nope.'

'Good,' Morgan said. 'So, if you weren't dressed appropriately for supper yesterday, do you have something appropriate you could wear tonight?'

He didn't give up did he? Carrie

wondered if she might be the first woman ever to refuse an invitation to eat with Morgan Harrington.

'If James won't punch me on the nose for asking,' Morgan added.

'He won't. He's not the jealous sort.'

'Good. Glad to hear it. So, supper?'

'I'm very busy.'

'So busy, you're standing here doodling?' Morgan raised a quizzical eyebrow at her.

'I'm waiting for the paint . . . '

'To dry?'

'Oh, very funny!' Despite her embarrassment at having been caught sketching Morgan, Carrie couldn't stop the laugh that escaped her lips. And it was with relief that she noticed Morgan had dropped the subject of joining him for supper. 'To be mixed, actually. And then I'm going to The Attic to source the paper.'

'Ah yes, that's something I want to discuss.'

Something seemed to have frozen suddenly in Morgan — his cheeky banter iced over in his throat. She was as sure that something sad — and possibly bad — had happened to this man, as she was as sure of her own name.

'Okay.'

Carrie tried to read the expression in Morgan's oh-so-beautiful eyes. Sadness? Regret? Longing? Or possibly a compilation of all three. Yesterday, he'd said he wasn't going to be sleeping in the master bedroom. Was he changing his mind? Perhaps they did need to talk.

The assistant arrived then with the cans of paint.

'You can put them in the boot of my car,' Morgan told him.

'No!' Carrie said. 'I can . . . '

Morgan laid a restraining hand on Carrie's arm — and again she got that bolt of electricity fizzing through her.

'It will save you lugging heavy cans up the steps if I'm not around when you arrive.'

'I'm used to carrying heavy things,' Carrie said. With a pang of pain she remembered carrying heavy boxes of wedding presents down to her car to take them back to the guests who had bought them, when Aaron walked out on her just days before their wedding.

'So which is it to be?' the assistant asked, with an amused smile.

'I'll make a deal,' Morgan said, turning to Carrie. 'The paint goes in your car if you agree to lunch with me, seeing as supper is off the agenda.'

'I haven't got time for lunch today. I . . .'

'Coffee then? Now? A crowded café somewhere? Is it a deal?'

'That's hardly a deal!'

'I missed breakfast to get here on time,' Morgan said.

Ouch — a reference to her having been late yesterday?

'Well . . . ' Carrie checked her watch. 'I might — '

'Listen,' the assistant said. 'I don't get paid to play wallflower around here. Could you two lovers sort out your problem somewhere else?'

'We're not lovers. We've only just met! We hardly — ' Carrie stopped speaking as she suddenly realised that, at that moment, what she wanted most in all the world was for Morgan to be her lover.

'In your car, I think,' Morgan said, and his smile reached his eyes and crinkled the sides.

Carrie nodded. Morgan had seen exactly what was in her mind, hadn't he? But she had to keep this relation-ship business-like at all costs.

So why did she hear herself say, 'There's an excellent café in Burston. It's on the way to The Attic.'

★ ★ ★

The Gardener's Glade was busier than Carrie had thought it would be. She and Morgan had to squeeze together into a space that was really only big enough for one.

Morgan cut his teacake — oozing with butter — into small squares and

31

picked up a piece and held it to Carrie's lips.

'Peace offering,' he said. 'Since I seem to have offended you by inviting you to supper!'

'You didn't offend me,' she said, holding his gaze. She didn't normally eat buttery things but she knew if she refused his peace offering then she could well offend him over that. And — she reminded herself — he still had the power to withdraw the contract for her to decorate his house.

She opened her mouth just wide enough for him to place the piece of teacake on her tongue.

'And they weren't rejections,' she said when she'd finished eating. 'It was just an inconvenient time to be asked, that's all.'

'Ah, so if I were to ask you another time? Saturday?'

'I can't do weekends,' Carrie replied, whippet fast. She looked down at her hands and began tidying the wands of sugar in the bowl.

'James?'

'Well, there's something I have to tell you . . . '

Morgan's mobile pinged then.

'Do you mind?' he asked Carrie, taking his phone from his jacket pocket.

'Not at all,' she said.

'*Bonjour*, Delphine. *Oui* . . . ' Morgan shrugged his shoulders and turned to Carrie. 'Excuse me,' he said, getting up. 'I'll take this call outside.'

When Morgan didn't come back, Carrie couldn't shake off a feeling of rejection and abandonment — not quite the same as when Aaron had jilted her, but it was so unexpected in its suddenness.

Whoever this Delphine was she was obviously important to Morgan, if he could run out on her like that. He sees me as a diversion, doesn't he? Carrie thought — I'm here and Delphine's not. The second he'd taken that call he hadn't been able to get out of the café quick enough.

After waiting ten minutes, Carrie went out to the car park but Morgan's silver Mercedes was nowhere to be seen.

★　★　★

Now, she pulled up outside The Attic, her mind in a whirl. The memory of how he'd held the piece of buttery teacake towards her as though they'd been lovers of long-standing and that he knew toasted teacake was her favourite thing in the whole world, sent a thrilling shiver through her. Delphine — whoever and whatever she was to him — hadn't been in Morgan's mind then, had she?

Carrie was about to get out of the car and go into The Attic when Morgan's number appeared in the window of her mobile.

'Carrie?'

'Yes.'

'Why the hell did you run out on me like that?'

'Why did *I* run out on *you*? It was the other way around!'

'I didn't run out on you. The signal was breaking up on my mobile, so I drove to the top of the hill to get a better one.'

'You could have let me know.'

'Carrie, it was a matter of seconds!'

'Ten minutes, actually. You're not the only one who doesn't like to be kept waiting,' Carrie said. 'If I'm going to finish this project on time, then time is of the essence. I'm in The Attic car park and I'm about to go in and source the wallpaper and fabrics. Do we go with stripes?'

'If you don't mind me saying so, Carrie, you sound a bit miffed.'

'Miffed? Why should I be? You can take calls from whoever you want.'

'Ah, so you are miffed. Delphine — '

'I am not miffed!'

'You are. You gave yourself away.'

'About what exactly?'

'Where shall I start?'

Carrie held the phone away from her

ear, not wanting to hear what explanation Morgan might be coming up with.

'I need to check my window measurements again,' Carrie interrupted before he could say anything. 'I've had another idea about how to dress the windows.'

Carrie was back in professional mode now — Delphine filed away in the part of her brain where she kept irrelevant thoughts.

'Call any time,' Morgan said. 'I'm going back to the Hall now.'

Morgan's voice purring in her ear was sending shivers of delight across her shoulders. Damn, damn, damn. Delphine, and whatever she was to Morgan, was mattering very much to Carrie indeed.

3

Luckily, Carrie saw the perfect paper almost right away, and less then two hours later her car scrunched to a halt on the gravel. Morgan's Mercedes was parked neatly in the corner by the hedge.

She unlocked the boot, pulled out a sample-roll of wallpaper, along with some fabric swatches for drapes, cushions and chair coverings she'd brought along. Then she strode purposefully up the steps.

She rang the bell. And waited. And waited and waited, the nervous flutter in the pit of her stomach rapidly changing to churning anxiety.

Morgan had to be here somewhere if his car was parked outside. Carrie turned the large brass doorknob.

It turned easily under her fingers.

'Morgan?' she called, stepping inside.

She put her things down on the tiled hall floor and closed the door behind her. 'Morgan?' she called again.

She listened hard to see if she could detect sound from somewhere in the house, but it was eerily silent. Morgan wouldn't have left a house like this, with so many valuable things inside, unlocked. Something had to be wrong.

She walked through to the drawing room but Morgan wasn't there. The kitchen, then?

The feeling of sadness Carrie had experienced when she'd first entered Oakenbury Hall was palpable now. She walked back out into the hall where portraits of Harrington forebears stared back at her in their ornate frames hanging from gilt hooks on the walls — a few gaps here and there but enough of them to tell her Morgan's family went back a long way.

And then she heard a sound — a chair being scraped across a stone floor? Cautiously, she walked down the long corridor towards the kitchen. The door was open, and across the room, sitting at the scrubbed pine table with his head in his hands, was Morgan.

'Morgan?' she said.

He jerked his head up and stared at her, his eyes wide with surprise.

'You might have knocked,' he snapped. He banged his hands down hard on the table, covering some paper.

'I rang the bell. Twice.'

'Not for long enough, obviously.'

'Then I'll know for next time, won't I?' It was obvious to Carrie that Morgan was upset about something. And he was probably embarrassed that she could see he was, which was why he'd snapped at her. 'Would you prefer it if I left? I can come back another time.'

'No. Come in. Sit down.'

Morgan gestured to the chair opposite him.

Carrie sat. She looked into eyes that were red-rimmed and puddled with tears. But still he was a handsome man — giving way to his feelings making

39

him more manly in Carrie's eyes. And she could forgive him for reacting the way he had, caught out with his emotions on display like trinkets in a gift shop.

'I'll make you a cup of tea,' Morgan said, his voice softer now.

He pushed himself off the chair but then flopped back down again. 'Whoops. I'm a bit giddy. Been sitting too long.'

'Shall *I* put the kettle on?' Carrie said.

'No. No, I'll do it.'

Morgan levered himself up from his sitting position, but when he picked up the kettle his hands were shaking so much he could hardly hold it under the running tap.

'I'll do it,' Carrie said, leaping up and prising the kettle from fingers that were warm and smooth.

What would it feel like to have those fingers cup her face? To have them running through her hair, and massaging her scalp gently? To have them glide over her arms, her back, her . . . Whoa, stop girl, Carrie told herself. This man abandoned you in a café, left you to pay the bill while he went to take a phone call from someone called Delphine — and whatever it was she had spoken to him about, it looked as though it'd upset him.

Slipping china mugs from their hooks on the dresser, Carrie poured the tea and handed Morgan the steaming drink.

But instead of taking it from her he wrapped his hands around hers, and held them fast. Poor Morgan — he looked like a small child, left alone for the first time. She wanted to put her arms around him, pull his head down on her shoulder and take away his pain — whatever that pain might be. And the most horrible part, thought Carrie, is that I hope his sadness has something to do with Delphine — that she's ended their relationship. Which would leave him free to take me to lunch or dinner or . . . no don't go there. Keep your thoughts professional.

'I've been expecting it for months now,' Morgan said.

When he didn't explain or continue, Carrie said, 'Delphine? Is the letter from Delphine? News you didn't want?'

'Delphine?' Morgan looked genuinely puzzled.

'The phone call you ran out on me to answer,' Carrie reminded him.

'I didn't run out on you. I went to get a signal. I told you. And for your information, Delphine works for me.'

In what sort of capacity? Carrie wondered. She couldn't imagine working with Morgan and not wanting to get even closer — as close as lovers do. Gosh, what was getting into her today?

He was so close — kissable close — his eyes fixed on hers.

'Sorry,' he said suddenly, looking away but as though he had to force himself to. 'I didn't mean to snap just now. You caught me at a low moment. I knew there'd be a letter for me from my father somewhere. I found it after lunch in the desk in his office — the secret drawer he knew I knew about at the back. I should have looked before. And there's a lump of guilt lodged around my heart that I didn't visit him as often as I should have done — could have done. I put business before him far more often than I ought to have done. He could have told me those things, face-to-face if only I'd made the effort to be here. I went straight back to Cannes after his funeral instead of coming here, being where he'd been so recently — his essence would still have been here. I wish I hadn't done that now.'

'We all have regrets,' Carrie said. And not the least of hers was that she'd given her own father such grief as a teenager and that she hadn't told him how much she'd loved him.

'I cut his phone calls short so many times,' Morgan went on, as though Carrie hadn't spoken. 'And he said, 'I'll write it all down for you, before I forget.' He made a joke of it, but he knew his memory was going and *I* knew he was hurt by my actions. But still I didn't visit because I was busy.' Morgan slid his hand across the pages of the letter. 'And now here it is. It's no good writing 'I love you' on a bunch of funeral flowers, Carrie. You have to tell people you love them when they're alive.'

Morgan took a deep breath and let it out in a sad sigh.

'Yes,' Carrie said, with difficulty, because it was as though Morgan knew she had that very regret.

'I haven't unloaded the paint yet. I went straight to the bureau. It was as though some other force was telling me to. And I've read it over and over so many times.'

Again, Morgan made to stand up but wobbled and slumped back down in his chair.

'How long have you been sitting here, reading?' Carrie asked.

'An hour? An hour and a half? I didn't think to time myself.'

Carrie sucked her breath in, surprised at his sharpness when she was only trying to help. But then, the poor man had had a massive emotional upset. She'd forgive him his rudeness — for now.

'No wonder you feel giddy if you've been here that long, with your head down, reading. And you're probably cold.'

'That too. Good tea, Carrie, thank you.'

Morgan touched Carrie briefly on the shoulder and a ripple of pure delight shot between her shoulder blades. Carrie gulped. How inappropriate to be getting the hots for someone when they were obviously in a state of distress.

'Did you ever meet my father by any chance?' Morgan asked.

'Your father? No. I've never met him.'

'Read that.' He thrust the pages of the letter at Carrie.

'Oh, I don't think . . . '

'Carrie. Read it,' he said, the amber

flecks in his eyes shooting arrows of reflected light towards Carrie from the sun that streamed through the window. She put a hand up to shield her eyes from the brightness. 'Please,' he added, when Carrie showed no intention of taking the letter from him. 'If we're going to be working together, you need to read it.'

If?

'Is it about Oakenbury Hall?'

'Yes.'

It didn't take long for Carrie to read the letter. Paintings missing from the walls had been sold to pay off gambling debts — someone called Talbot. There were words of regret that he hadn't been more supportive to Morgan over Georgina. '*Oakenbury Hall is not to be sold out of the family!!!*' Carrie read. And — heavily underlined — was what, to Carrie, looked like an order rather than a wish . . . that Morgan would marry so that the house could be passed to his children.

So, that was why he thought she had

spoken to his father — because she had said this was a house that needed children in it.

'You and my father were thinking along the same lines.'

'It would seem so.' Carrie said.

'And do you still think this house needs children in it?'

'I do.'

'That's what I like about you, Carrie — you don't say what you think I want to hear. You speak from the heart. And you don't try to wriggle out of things.'

'Who are Talbot and Georgina?' she asked, changing the subject, because her heart was doing some very funny bunny-hops right now.

Morgan finished his mug of tea. He stood up and held out a hand towards Carrie. But instead of taking hold of it, Carrie roughly stuffed her hands inside her trouser pockets. She felt compassion for Morgan's situation, of course she did, but what sort of a fool would she be if she let him take advantage of that compassion? Holding hands could be such an intimate thing to do. And there was still Delphine in the equation, wasn't there?

'Please, Carrie,' Morgan said, his hand still held out towards her. 'Come into the drawing room with me and I'll tell you — it's warmer in there. And besides, I've got no one else I can tell.'

And despite her misgivings, and because Carrie knew what it was to be alone, she placed her hand in his and walked with him down the corridor to the drawing room. But she was under no illusion that she was anything more to Morgan than a convenient hand to hold.

4

'I don't believe this!'

Try as she might, Carrie's car wouldn't start. The boot was laden with paint and her brushes, and all the other things she needed to make a start on the master bedroom. And her pasting boards and step-ladder were strapped to the roof. The damned car just *had* to start — she'd promised Morgan she'd begin today.

Morgan's revelation that his brother Talbot had stolen his fiancée, Georgina, from him had touched a nerve with Carrie — her own ex-fiancé, Aaron, had left her for her best friend. She'd almost told Morgan the whole sorry story but decided against it — Morgan didn't need to hear about similar situations when his own was obviously still so painful to him.

'How could you, James!' she yelled as

the engine refused to kick into life.

She got out, and slammed the door shut. She would have to see if she could hire a car, or a van, from somewhere. And fast.

But first she would have to tell Morgan she was going to be late — again. She was not looking forward to it one bit. She tapped in his number.

'Good morning, Carrie,' he said before the sound of her tapping had died in her ears, as though he'd been waiting for her to call. 'What's the problem?'

'Did I say there was a problem?'

'No. But I have a hunch there is one. Don't tell me . . . that wreck of a car of yours won't start?'

'It's just a little hitch.'

'So I was right! The car's kaput?'

'I'm just having trouble getting it started, that's all,' she said. 'I'll give it one more go and then I'll ring around car hire firms. I've got the numbers here.'

'No need,' Morgan said. 'I have to come into Farchester anyway. I'll pick you up in, say, forty minutes?'

'My flat might be a bit difficult to find, so I think hiring is going to be best.'

'Satnav, Carrie? Ever heard of it?'

'Of course I have!'

Not that she had one herself.

'Well then, I'm going to be able to find you, aren't I? And really, it's not out of my way.'

'Well, if you're sure.'

'I am. And it's the least I can do after you listened to all my woes the other day. See you soon.'

And before Carrie had a chance to reply Morgan killed the call, and she was left standing, quivering slightly from the things his voice was doing to her body. Even though she knew she'd only been a convenient shoulder to — literally — cry on for Morgan. Delphine hadn't been there and she had. That was the only reason Morgan was being so understanding now.

Oh why did life have to be so complicated sometimes?

★　★　★

Carrie was sitting on the front door-step, already dressed in her overalls, when Morgan pulled up at the kerb. Paste boards, a ladder, pots of paint and a bag with rolls of wallpaper sticking out of it were piled up beside her.

'Hi,' he said, opening the car door.

Carrie leapt to her feet, picked up the paste boards and the black plastic sack and hurried towards his car. Morgan immediately sprang into action and helped her load her things into his Mercedes.

'Sorry about all this,' Carrie said as she settled into the passenger seat, sliding her hands over the edge of it, getting herself comfortable. How luxurious it felt and smelled; it was the smell of a very expensive car. 'Oh, I'm not going to damage this lovely leather with my overalls, am I?'

'Not unless the paint on your overalls is still wet.'

Carrie dabbed at a paint-spattered trouser leg.

'Nope,' she said. 'And don't worry — I won't have to ask you to do this again because I've got a small van hired for tomorrow morning.'

'Good,' Morgan said. 'That rust bucket of yours is going nowhere, is it? Did you know the exhaust is falling off?'

'Excuse me! How dare you call James a rust bucket! I'm very fond of him, you know.'

'James is your car?' Morgan said. Then he burst out laughing. 'No wonder he wasn't likely to punch me on the nose for inviting you to dinner.'

'Yes, James is my car. Silly to give a car a name, I know, but I did and I hope the garage can mend him. I've asked them to deliver it to your house if it's ready later today.'

'And if it isn't?'

'I was rather hoping you might be able to give me a lift back as well. Or . . .'

'Or what, Carrie?'

'Or I could get a taxi.'

'Taxis will eat into your profit margin.'

'I know. What with the hired van costs as well. But doing some of the work myself instead of contracting out should see me through. And I can offset the costs on my tax return, can't I?'

'You can. But I've got a better idea,' Morgan said.

'What's that?'

'You could throw a few overnight things in a bag and stop?'

Carrie looked at him, and then glanced towards her car. She fiddled with the buttons on her overalls, adjusting the buckles on the bib part.

'I think I've got to face facts, Morgan. James is done for really, isn't he?'

Morgan nodded.

'And I can't tell you how pleased I am about that.'

'That's not a nice thing to say,' Carrie said. 'You can probably just go out and buy another car, but I can't.'

'I think we're talking at cross purposes,' Morgan said, grinning at her.

'Are we?' Carrie said. She thought she'd heard Morgan ask her to stop the night but what with the stress of James breaking down, and being behind with the job already, she couldn't be sure.

'So will you?' Morgan said.

'Will I what?'

'Stop over?'

'Um . . . '

'I could help strip wallpaper or something. I'm not completely useless as a male of the species.'

'I've got a vapour stripper,' Carrie said.

All this talk of stripping — and in such close proximity to Morgan — was making her feel hot. She tugged at the neck of her T-shirt. But she could see that stopping the night at Oakenbury Hall would mean she'd be able to get a steal on the job. And get a feel for the house.

'I could stop,' Carrie said. 'But not if,

you know, me stopping will make things difficult with you and Delphine.'

'Delphine? My colleague?'

Morgan looked, Carrie thought, genuinely puzzled for some reason.

'Yes. Her.'

'Well, you can take it from me: Delphine isn't going to mind. Delphine is gay. She lives with her girlfriend.'

'Good. Won't be a mo, then,' Carrie said.

Goodness, how deliciously relieved that little bit of information had made her. She threw open the car door, leapt out and ran back to her flat to shove a few things for an overnight stop in a bag.

★   ★   ★

The vaporised paper stripper made short work of taking off the old paper so she hadn't needed Morgan's help. He busied himself in his study sorting out family papers.

I could murder a cup of tea right

now, Carrie thought. There was a bell-pull thing in the corner — if she were to pull it would a servant miraculously appear? Carrie giggled — ringing a bell to get someone to make her a cup of tea for goodness' sake!

'Oh, there you are . . . oh my God, what happened?' Carrie jumped in surprise as Morgan suddenly appeared in the doorway. Deep in thought, she hadn't heard him coming up the stairs.

Morgan had blood streaked across his cheek, and there was a gash on the top of one hand.

'I fell. I think it must be years since anyone has been in the barn.' Morgan put a hand to his forehead and swayed slightly.

'What were you doing in the barn?'

'Looking for a ladder. The ceilings are higher in here than on the ground floor.'

Carrie pointed to her extendable ladder, already raised to ceiling height.

'Not much. I've reached this ceiling

easily enough. Thanks for looking but it looks as though you're bleeding to death needlessly.'

'Am I?' Morgan said. He put his hand on top of his head.

Carrie leapt to catch him. She stifled a giggle because wasn't it always the big men who fainted at the sight of blood? — Morgan was just playing true-to-type, and it wasn't as if it was gallons of the stuff. She grabbed his arm by the wrist and pulled him towards the bed. Not quite the scenario she'd imagined herself having with Morgan a short while ago as she'd covered the satin quilt with the dust-sheets.

Pushing him onto the bed, Carrie pressed Morgan's head down towards his knees.

'Oh God, sorry, I've got paint on your jeans.'

Morgan didn't answer, merely groaned, so Carrie kept her hand on the back of his neck, smoothing his skin, willing him not to pass out completely. How blond his hair was so close up, how thick. Carrie resisted the urge to run her fingers through it — the place might have been right, but the timing was definitely way off. And anyway, what would be the point? Carrie Fraser from Flat Two, Laurel House, wouldn't even be on the longlist of possibles for the role of Mrs Morgan Harrington. Not that she wanted to be because she had a business to build up and a career to get off the ground first.

'I don't want to move,' Morgan said, just as Carrie was beginning to wonder if they were going to have to spend the rest of the day sitting like this. 'Mmm, that's nice.'

'What is?'

'Your neck-massaging technique.'

Carrie immediately pulled her hand away.

'If you're winding me up about this,' she said, 'I'll — '

'You'll what?' Morgan righted himself and looked at her.

They were so close — kissing close. Carrie was certain Morgan would be able to hear her hastening heartbeat.

'I'll put iodine on that cut instead of tea tree oil and give you something to really groan about!'

'You wouldn't?'

'Try me,' Carrie teased.

She got up and fetched her first aid kit, which she carried everywhere when she was working.

'Good heavens, you've got everything in there,' Morgan said as she rifled through it looking for swabs, dressings and the tea tree oil. 'Actually, the cuts aren't so bad, but I did knock myself out for a few moments.'

'Right.' Carrie said. She grabbed a small torch. 'I'll have to check for concussion. I'm insured against injuries to myself or other parties while I'm working. And I'm up to date on my first aid certificates. Back on the bed.'

Back on the bed . . . had she really said that?

'Anything you say, nurse,' Morgan said, grinning broadly.

Hmmm, Carrie thought as she

checked Morgan for concussion — he was fine — and took his pulse, which seemed to be deep and slow and regular. She wondered what her own pulse was like right now and she prayed Morgan wouldn't jokingly suggest he take it.

'You'll live,' Carrie said. She ripped open a swab sachet and cleaned Morgan's wound. 'I think the air will heal that more quickly than any creams.'

'You sound like you know what you're talking about.'

'My father was a doctor.'

'Was?'

'He died when I was sixteen.'

It had been a horrible time, but almost another sixteen years had passed since then — she'd lived as many years without her father as with him.

'I'm sorry,' Morgan said. He touched Carrie briefly on the back of her wrist. 'I expect you'll think I'm losing it, but I thought I heard my father calling my name as I was coming round in the barn.'

'You're not losing it,' Carrie said. 'There's lots we don't understand. Lots we'll never know about.'

There was a moment's silence between them, a heartbeat — yet for Carrie it was a comfortable silence, as though at that precise time they were both on the exact same wavelength. She smiled at Morgan encouragingly, but he grinned back.

'You've got paint on the end of your nose,' he said. 'Did you know?'

Carrie's hand flew to her nose, but Morgan grabbed it.

'You'll only make it spread — you can't see where exactly.'

'Morgan,' Carrie said, 'I know where my nose is and doing the job I do, a bit of paint here and there is par for the course.'

Still holding Carrie's hand, Morgan took a fresh swab from the packet and wiped the paint away. And Carrie let him without protest; she loved the feeling of someone caring enough to do it for her. A lump came to her throat, and threatened to choke her. Morgan was looking down at her, and she couldn't take her eyes away. He was oh-so-kissable close again. But he was only flirting with her, wasn't he? A man like him, so good-looking, so rich, so charismatic, probably did this sort of thing on automatic pilot. It would mean nothing to him if she were to reach up and kiss his full, beautifully shaped mouth. It would be a short hop and skip until the dust-sheets were whisked off the bed and they were in it and he was making — probably very expert — love to her.

'A nursery, Carrie,' Morgan said, startling Carrie back to reality. 'Can you add that to your brief?'

'A nursery?' Carrie almost choked on the word. 'Babies or flowers?'

'Oh, I think you know which.'

'Which room?' Carrie squeaked.

'You choose,' Morgan said.

'Next to this one, I think,' Carrie said, immediately going into professional mode again. 'I wouldn't want my children down the end of a long corridor.'

And that was another thing — the corridor would need to be painted in a much lighter shade than the mid-green it was now — a rather nauseating mid-green in Carrie's opinion. And more lighting was needed. As far as Carrie could remember, offhand, there was only one light at each end of the corridor — and high up. Wall lights would look good. Hmm, she could do so much with this house, given free rein and a decent budget.

'You wouldn't? Is that a personal or professional answer?'

'Personal. People who own houses like this probably want their children miles away and with someone else to look after them.'

'Don't put us all in the same box, Carrie,' Morgan interrupted. 'But as it happens, I agree with you. The room next to this one it is then.'

Morgan gave Carrie the benefit of his megawatt smile and her heart flipped over.

'I think,' Carrie said, her voice husky

with desire, 'I'd better get on, don't you?'

'Yes,' Morgan said, and Carrie couldn't help noticing that his voice was just as husky, if deeper. 'I think it would be for the best if you did. I'll call you when supper's ready.'

⋆ ⋆ ⋆

'In here?' Carrie asked.

She peered around the doorway. The dining room table was set with what looked to her like a cupboard full of crockery and cutlery. It was all gleaming in light cast from a massive candelabra on the table — too many candles for her to count from where she stood. This was by far the nicest room she'd seen in the house so far. There were half a dozen or so still lifes — all of fruit or flowers — on the walls, all top-lit by strip lights. The walls themselves were painted a deepish maroon which gave the room an intimate feel.

Too intimate for Carrie at that moment.

'Why not in here?' Morgan said. 'It's where we eat in Oakenbury Hall.'

'All the time? Breakfast, lunch, everything?'

'Well, not breakfast except at weekends. But then, yes — breakfast is always served here.'

Morgan gestured for Carrie to walk on through.

'But I'm still in my overalls. I can't eat in here in overalls.'

'As you see, I'm wearing what I've been wearing all day and haven't changed for dinner.' Morgan made an ushering gesture but Carrie stayed where she was.

'No,' Carrie said, taking in Morgan's jeans, still with the blob of paint from when she'd been seeing to his cuts, and his blue and white fine-striped shirt, open at the neck, revealing a few blond hairs that she had an urge to reach out and tuck away for him. 'But you still look a lot smarter and cleaner than I am.'

'If it makes you feel better you can go

and change. Dinner won't spoil.'

Change? All Carrie had brought with her was clean underwear, and something to sleep in — her oldest winter PJs at that because she'd noticed the heating hadn't been on in Oakenbury Hall when she'd come to do the estimate. Underneath her overalls she was wearing an ancient pair of very faded navy combats and a T-shirt that had once been bright raspberry but had faded to a shade closer to raspberry milkshake, it had been through the wash so many times.

'I didn't think dinner would be so, well, *dressy*,' Carrie said. 'I've only got what I'm standing up in, more or less.' She lifted one leg of her overalls to reveal her combats underneath.

Morgan smiled.

'You look fine to me. But if it makes you feel better then I'm sure there's a dress, er . . . someone . . . left behind somewhere . . . ' His voice trailed away.

Georgina's dress, no doubt, Carrie thought — no way was she going to wear his ex-lover's dress.

'It's okay,' Carrie said. 'I've decided I'm fine as I am.'

'Then come and sit. I'll be waiter, chef and host all rolled into one tonight.'

He waved towards the dresser and a cut glass bowl full to the brim with fresh fruit salad — her favourite dessert.

'Who . . . '

'Me.'

Carrie laughed.

'But we're never going to eat our way through that lot! Well, not tonight.'

'Okay,' Morgan said, 'so I overestimated the quantity. You can have some for breakfast too. But you'll have to forgive me. I'm your stereotypical spoilt little rich boy who's never made so much as a sandwich before.'

'But,' Carrie said, 'you made it for me?'

'Yes. Now come and eat.'

'I'll, um, just take my overalls off then,' Carrie said.

She unzipped them, and holding on to the door frame for support, she stepped out of them, draped them over a chair in the hall — all the time conscious that Morgan was watching her. She felt exposed, naked, and yet it wasn't an uncomfortable feeling.

'And I'd better take my hat off.'

She pulled off the baseball cap she always wore when decorating, and her hair — which she'd bundled roughly on top of her head — tumbled down. She shook her head to loosen the strands and ran her fingers through it.

'Chestnuts,' Morgan said.

Carrie pulled a face. She hated chestnuts, even in stuffing at Christmas. She hoped against hope he wasn't going to serve her chestnuts.

'Er, is there something else?' she said. Time for a little white lie. 'To eat, I mean. I'm allergic to chestnuts.'

Morgan made a strange sort of sound — somewhere between the beginnings of a laugh and a low growl.

'Not to eat,' he said — rather huskily

Carrie thought. 'Your hair as you shook it out reminded me of chestnuts, fresh from their prickly cases.'

'Phew! That's all right then,' Carrie said.

Morgan smiled at her.

'Dinner,' he said, 'without chestnuts, is served.'

He made a v of his arm and Carrie slipped her hand through it, and he led her to her seat at one end of the table. She was so close to tears now — so moved that Morgan had gone to so much trouble for her. She would have to eat as much of it as she could, and with good grace — whatever it tasted like.

★   ★   ★

'That was delicious,' Carrie said.

'Apart from the rather rustic fruit salad, I can't take any credit, I'm afraid,' Morgan said. 'Mrs Dawkins keeps a full freezer, always.'

'Mrs Dawkins?'

'My late father's housekeeper. She's in Bristol visiting her sister at the moment.'

Carrie smiled at him as he began to refill her glass with the best white wine she'd ever tasted.

'Whoa!' she said, putting a hand over the top of her glass. The last thing she wanted was to drink too much and make a fool of herself. Right now, Morgan looked like a Michelangelo angel, or a Greek statue, with the flickery, soft candlelight highlighting his blondness.

'Penny for them,' Morgan said. 'You were miles away.'

'Oh, they're worth a bit more than that,' Carrie said. She peered into her drink, afraid to catch Morgan's eye in case he saw her longing for him in them.

'Nightcap?' Morgan said and Carrie thought he sounded nervous.

'No thanks. I've drunk enough already. And the food was delicious. Thank you.'

'It was no trouble. The table and all the paraphernalia on it was here, the food was in the freezer, the wine in the cellar.'

He hadn't gone to any trouble just for her, had he? It was of no consequence to Morgan, was it? She'd been stupid to be so touched by it.

'I think I'll get an early night,' Carrie said. She swallowed the last of her wine.

'Carrie, it's only half past nine! Was it something I said?'

'No, of course not. I've been very busy today, as you know, and I'm tired. And I need to think what I'm going to do about getting another car, and . . . '

'Carrie. Stop.'

Morgan got up from his chair on the opposite side of the table to Carrie and came to sit beside her. He prised her hands off the glass she knew she was clinging to like a life-raft. Then he took her hands in his and held them. And it felt good, so good — almost treacherously good.

'I'm still going to have an early night,'

Carrie said. She wriggled her hands from Morgan's.

'Why?'

'I've just told you.'

'It's more than that, isn't it?'

Carrie pressed her lips together because she couldn't trust herself to speak. Socially, they were poles apart, weren't they? Oh, she wasn't so naive as to not know which knife and fork to use or any of that sort of thing, but there would be differences — if not a chasm — between them always. Besides, she'd yet to tell him about her mother and the care she would need for the rest of her life. And yet she was drawn to him in a way she'd never really been drawn to Aaron, she knew that now.

Carrie pushed back her chair, but Morgan leapt to his feet to hold it for her.

'Well then, Carrie, if I can't tempt you to a nightcap then I'll say goodnight.'

Morgan placed his hands on her shoulders and Carrie felt herself freeze, but in the same instant Morgan kissed the top of her head and she melted again.

'I have never, ever, forced a woman to do something she didn't want to do, and I'm not going to start now.'

'I'll see you in the morning,' Carrie said, her voice a whisper as she summoned every last ounce of her self-control.

5

Carrie was up, showered and dressed for work, by 7 a.m. She listened for any sound of Morgan moving around anywhere, but all she could hear was birdsong drifting through the fanlight window she'd left open all night.

How peaceful it was here — a world away from her flat on a busy street.

Through apple trees just coming into blossom, Carrie could see the shimmer of light on water in the distance. A river perhaps, or maybe a lake. She had a sudden urge to be outside: to smell the blossom, to walk across the massive expanse of grass and feel it soft beneath her feet.

She opened the bedroom door and peeped out onto the landing. Which one of the bedrooms was Morgan's? It had been impossible to tell on the tour of the house he'd given her — and he hadn't said. And there hadn't been the tell-tale sign of a shirt hanging up anywhere, or shoes kicked off and left lying where they'd fallen. Or a photo of a special someone in a frame on a bedside table in any of the rooms. It was as though he wasn't intending to stop long this time, just as he'd not come to see his father often either. Cannes was his main home and he'd be going back soon — why leave personal stuff lying about?

In the kitchen, Carrie tried turning the knob of the back door and to her surprise it creaked open. Perhaps Morgan was up after all. But there was no sign that he'd been in the kitchen. Carrie turned back into the room and put her hand to the kettle but it was cold.

Granite worktops, Carrie said to herself, would work in here. But nothing too modern — no stainless steel, no glass. Elm, perhaps, to replace the white-painted cupboard doors.

She ran a hand over the domed

chrome lids of the Aga. Cold. As though the poor thing hadn't been lit, or loved, in a long while.

'But you can stay,' she told it, 'if I'm asked to do up this room.'

Then she stepped outside into the garden and inhaled deeply, the air fresh and surprisingly warm for so early in the morning, and made her way across the grass. There was a circular seat around one of the apple trees — wrought iron, rather rusty with lichen attached here and there. Carrie sat down and reached up to pull a branch of blossom towards her. She closed her eyes and sniffed — mmmm, it smelled good. Then her hand found its way to the top of her head where Morgan had kissed her the night before.

'Ah, there you are.'

Morgan's voice startled her. Had he known by her gesture that she'd been remembering?

'Oh! I hope you don't mind me, you know, taking liberties coming into your garden.'

'Of course not,' he said walking towards her carrying two mugs of tea. He was wearing a dressing-gown, but his legs, peeping from the bottom of it, were bare.

Was he, Carrie wondered, wearing anything at all underneath that dressing-gown? She could hardly drag her eyes away from it.

'Thanks,' Carrie said, taking the tea from him and wrapping her hands around the mug. Better that than unfastening the belt of his dressing-gown which was what she really wanted to do.

'Sleep well?' Morgan asked.

'Very, thank you. It's so quiet here.' Carrie looked around the garden at the tulips just beginning to open their petals as the sun crept higher in the sky, and other flowers she didn't know the names of. 'I think I'm in love with this house.'

'Are you?' Morgan said — something like shock in his voice.

'You sound as if you aren't,' Carrie said.

And the minute the words were out of her mouth she could have bitten them back.

'Do I?'

'A bit,' she said. 'But sorry — it's not in my brief to offer opinions.'

'It's okay. Don't apologise.' Morgan sipped his tea and swallowed.

Carrie watched his Adam's apple going up and down. He hadn't shaved yet, and she was surprised to see that the stubble on his neck and chin was darker than his hair. Surprised and rather thrilled because it gave him a rakish air — not quite as bandbox fresh as he had been. What would it be like to wake up beside him each morning and have his stubbled chin brush her cheek?

'I'm still trying to decide what to do about the house actually,' Morgan said, cutting through her daydreams.

'Oh! So why have you brought me in?'

'Cosmetic job initially. Tidy it up a bit prior to selling. But now I've found my father's letter expressing his wishes that I don't sell, it will still be cosmetic only for renting out.'

'Expensive cosmetics,' Carrie said, softly. She couldn't imagine how he could possibly bear to get rid of a house as lovely as this. 'If it were me . . . '

'Well it's not.'

Carrie shuddered — she'd allowed her personal feelings to overstep her professional ones again, and Morgan hadn't much liked it. Don't bite the hand that feeds you, Carrie admonished herself, pressing her lips together.

'I've got a villa in Cannes and a business to run, after all.' Morgan stared into the distance.

'So, is the nursery project still on?' Carrie asked. It seemed pointless for Morgan to go to the expense of a nursery when whoever rented Oakenbury Hall might not need, or want, it.

Morgan didn't answer for what seemed like an eternity. Carrie's imagination began to run away with her and she saw her fee for this project going down the pan.

Why, oh why, couldn't she keep her mouth shut?

'Or there's my third option. I could leave your friend Genifer, and Jean-Claude, to run my business and move back here and let my future children grow up surrounded by countryside.'

'So, you're engaged to someone?'

'Did I say that?'

'No. You don't *have* to be engaged or married to have children.'

'You said that as though that wasn't how you'd do things. Not marry, I mean.'

'It's how I was brought up,' Carrie said. 'And it's how I'd want to raise a family — within a marriage.'

But if Morgan wasn't going to be marrying Delphine as she'd thought he was, then who *was* he thinking of having children with? There must be another woman in his life . . .

'That's me told!' Morgan laughed.

'Do you have to make a decision right away?' she asked. 'About the house.'

'Soonish,' Morgan said. 'But first

breakfast. Toast? Or there might be some eggs somewhere. I think I could just about scramble some eggs.'

'Toast will be fine, thanks. I don't want to put you to too much trouble.'

'You're not. More tea when the toast is done? I'll give you a shout.'

'Please,' Carrie said, but Morgan was already striding back towards the kitchen.

★ ★ ★

'Do you sail?' Morgan asked.

He'd made more toast than Carrie was ever going to be able to eat and was buttering a piece. He slid it onto a plate and handed it to Carrie.

'I went on the ferry to Calais once, when I was at school,' Carrie said. She cut her toast into neat fingers without looking up. 'Does that count?'

'But you didn't like it much — right?'

'I was sick before the ferry even slipped its moorings or whatever it is boats do. But it might have been the gin and orange my friends and I drank when Miss Keyte was fussing around with our passports.' Carrie grinned conspiratorially at him at the memory of it. 'Oh, and the duty free chocolate probably didn't help my cause either. We really were pretty smashed!'

'But you've never tried it again, er, less toxically challenged?'

Carrie laughed.

'That's a very polite way of putting it! But no. Never.'

'Any reason?'

Slowly, Carrie spread marmalade on a small square of toast.

'Did Genifer never tell you about . . . about . . . Aaron?'

'She didn't. I hired Gen and Jean-Claude because they are both discreet. Did she tell you anything personal about me?'

'No. Never.'

'Well then, it figures she wouldn't tell me about you.'

'Sounds like Gen,' Carrie said. 'Aaron and I were engaged. The wedding never happened.'

'I'm sorry. Really sorry. We've got a lot in common it seems. So, back to my sailing question. Is there any way you could be convinced to try it again?'

'I think I've been off the water too long to venture on it again, Morgan. I'm wary.'

'Well, you've come to the right person to lay that ghost. There's a dinghy . . . '

Carrie raised her shoulders up to the level of her ears and then dropped them again.

'I'm not really talking about dinghies.' she said.

'You're not?'

'No.'

'Carrie,' Morgan said, 'to use another nautical term, I'm a bit out of my depth here. I'm afraid I'm a mere bloke who doesn't read these things well.'

'I'm sorry. I'm talking in riddles, aren't I?'

Morgan nodded.

'A bit. I'll help if I can though.'

'Jumping straight in then,' Carrie said, 'seeing as we're talking all things water. I was jilted. Not quite at the altar, but near enough. We had the honeymoon booked — everything. We were going to stop in Gen and Jean-Claude's place, and they were going to stop in my flat while we were there. Except ... ' She folded her napkin, rolled it, and threaded it back through the holder.

'Except?'

'Aaron texted me two days before the ceremony. But I should have known because however many times Gen had asked us over before, Aaron didn't want to go. So, we never did. I thought his reluctance to take holidays was because we were saving for a place of our own, but in Aaron's case it seems it was his reluctance for us to have any sort of a future, anywhere, because he was two-timing me and he wanted his future to be with *her*.' Carrie banged her napkin in its holder down on the table, as though she was bringing the conversation to an end. She'd already said too much. 'Texted you?'

'And I texted back. I should have gone and told him face-to-face what I thought of him, but I didn't. Weak of me, wasn't it?'

'Weak?' Morgan said. 'I wouldn't say you were weak. Then or ever.'

'You're being very kind,' Carrie said, with a shrug of her shoulders. Rule one, never talk about your ex with someone you fancy — and she'd just broken that rule, big time. 'But I know I can't go on blaming Aaron for everything, forever. Another reason I don't do boats is that I can't swim.'

'You can't swim?'

'No.'

'I can't believe it.' Morgan shook his head in disbelief.

'There *are* people who can't swim, you know. And besides, I can do other things.'

Carrie picked up her mug and drained the last drops of tea.

'Like?' Morgan asked.

'I can draw as you found out in Greenbase. And I paint portraits in my spare time — sell them too. I played violin in the school orchestra and can probably still scratch out a tune. Oh, and I can tap dance. Eat your heart out Ginger Rogers style.'

'You're quite the accomplished young lady, then? But remember never to ask me to dance. My size thirteens would crush you.'

'I will,' Carrie said. She took her mug over to the sink and rinsed it under the tap. 'Finished?' she said, indicating his now empty mug.

And when Morgan nodded, she took that and rinsed it out too, then wiped both mugs and hung them back on their hooks on the dresser. How comfortably domestic this all was? She was as at home here in Morgan's kitchen as she was in her own.

But it could be dangerous to get too comfortable — she had been hired to do a job, that was all.

'And now I'd better get on,' she said.

★ ★ ★

Carrie crept quietly down the stairs to the kitchen. The time for lunch had been and gone hours ago and now she was starving — her tummy rumbling noisily. But the master bedroom was beginning to take shape nicely — all the woodwork was painted and the walls sized ready for the paper. And the making of the drapes was well in hand at The Attic.

From now on it would be only a matter of popping back now and then to check that her electrical contractors were getting on with work in the drawing room, and that everything else was running to schedule. And that Morgan was pleased with progress. She still had to do a mood board for the nursery Morgan said was now in his plans for Oakenbury Hall. She would need to get on with that soon — run her ideas past Morgan and get his approval.

She wondered where he might be

right now. A couple of hours after that horribly embarrassing breakfast, when she'd almost broken down telling him about Aaron, he'd shouted up the stairs that he was going out and would be back later. She was to help herself to anything she could find in the fridge or the larder.

So now she was going to do just that. And then she'd take whatever she found and a mug of tea out into the garden. And draw — with a pencil in her hand and something to concentrate on would stop her thoughts straying to all sorts of fancies where Morgan Harrington was concerned.

But despite finding a seat well away from where she'd drunk tea under the apple trees with Morgan earlier, her best efforts to draw the garden and the house from that perspective didn't happen. The only thing to fly from her fingers onto the paper was Morgan's profile.

Carrie sighed — her heart was well and truly ruling her head at the moment. She leaned back against the warm wall. She'd have to get back to work soon, but another five minutes, her face turned to the sun, feeling the peace of Morgan's garden soothe her — the first time she'd felt soothed in a long time — wouldn't hurt, would it?

Carrie must have dozed for a few minutes because she was startled suddenly by the sound of voices coming from the other side of the high stone wall. Morgan. And a woman. Mrs Dawkins back from visiting her sister? To move now would mean they might know she was there — but to stay and listen . . . she didn't really hold with eavesdropping.

'You, settling down? I'd never thought I'd see the day,' the woman said. 'Not the way my Ken says you've played the field, I didn't!'

'And there's me thinking I've been discreet,' Morgan laughed. 'Not that I've played the field in quite the way your husband might imagine! Anyway, I haven't settled yet.'

'There's still a question mark over it, then?'

'I haven't asked her, and besides . . . ' Morgan stopped speaking, and even from the other side of the wall Carrie could hear the sadness in his voice.

'No, and I don't suppose it'll come easy after what that minx Georgina did to you. And as for your brother . . . '

'No, it won't. Still, it's hypothetical at the moment.'

'Oh yes,' the woman laughed. 'Nurseries hypothetical, are they?'

Morgan laughed with her.

'It was one of those blindingly obvious moments. Suddenly I couldn't wait to see a child, children, in my old dinghy on the lake. But, d'you know, Carrie . . . '

'Is that her name? The one you're thinking of marrying?'

'Carrie's the interior decorator, Mrs Dawkins. Carrie can't swim. Can you imagine — me and my aquatic lifestyle with a wife who can't swim?'

But Carrie didn't wait to hear what

Mrs Dawkins' answer would be, or what Morgan was going to say next. She'd heard quite enough. Of course, a man as handsome and as rich as Morgan Harrington would have had more than his fair share of women — but it shouldn't be making her feel jealous, for goodness' sake! And hadn't he just made it perfectly clear that a woman who couldn't swim wouldn't even get within reach of his radar?

Back to work, my girl, Carrie chided herself. She scooped up her drawings and her pencils and her mug and plate and ran for the house. Closing the back door, Carrie leant against it, out of breath.

⋆ ⋆ ⋆

'I hope you've taken a break, Carrie,' Morgan said, leaning against the doorway of the master bedroom.

'Of course I've taken a break,' she said. 'In the garden actually. Fresh air, sunshine, that sort of thing.'

Carrie carried on trimming the end of a length of wallpaper as she spoke, her movements swift, controlled, accurate. But she didn't look up. She'd leave it up to him to work out whether he'd been overheard talking to Mrs Dawkins or not.

'That's very impressive — what you're doing. I'm all fingers and thumbs with anything practical.'

'Unless it's to do with yachts obviously. Or boats, or whatever they are.'

'Most of us are good at something, Carrie,' Morgan said.

Carrie grabbed a brush and began smoothing bubbles from the bottom of the length of wallpaper she'd finished trimming.

'Oh, and by the way,' Morgan said. 'I'm pretty pleased with progress so far.'

'Thank you,' Carrie said, twisting to look at him, giving him the briefest of professional smiles, before returning to the task in hand. 'I've not had any complaints yet. But we'll need a chat about the finer details for the nursery soon. Although I'm not sure it's the right thing to have me choose the colour scheme.' Carrie put down her brush and looked up at him again. 'I mean, the woman you're going to have children with will want to do that, I should think.'

'You do?'

'Definitely.'

'Well, we won't talk about that now. It's too lovely an evening to be working, Carrie,' Morgan said. 'So why don't we go over to the lake and watch the sunset?'

'I don't think so,' she said. 'My hire van should have been here by now.'

'Have you tried ringing them?'

'No signal,' Carrie said, tapping the phone in her pocket.

'Come and use the landline then.'

'I suppose I could . . . '

Carrie followed him out onto the landing and down the stairs.

But it was not good news for Carrie when the van hire firm eventually answered. And she let them know just what she thought of their ineptitude.

'There's been some sort of double-booking mess-up,' she said, finding Morgan in the kitchen. 'A van's not available until 7 o'clock. And it won't be here until 8 o'clock. It better had be!'

'Or you'll have their guts for garters!'

'You heard me?'

'Very impressive!

Carrie laughed.

'Honestly, what a way to run a business!'

'Indeed. Talking of which, I'll have to get back to mine soon.'

'When?'

'Saturday.'

'But that's the day after tomorrow.'

'It is. So, as I don't renege on promises unless it's a matter of life and death, Saturday it has to be. Just for the weekend. My plane goes at 5.30 a.m. In less than two hours after that I'll be breakfasting on fresh croissants. You could come with me if you like?'

'I don't think so.'

'Just throw a change of clothes in a bag. I'm sure you could stop with Genifer and Jean-Claude. They'd love to have you. You know, if it would make you feel more comfortable stopping with them rather than at my villa, seeing as we've only just met — as you so forcefully told the assistant in the paint shop.'

Morgan grinned at her but Carrie didn't grin back. He was laughing at her, wasn't he? Or teasing her at the very least. And she didn't like being teased. Not at the moment anyway.

'It's not that, Morgan,' she told him. 'Honestly. I can't do weekends. I told you.'

'And you're not going to tell me why?'

Carrie shook her head.

Morgan shrugged his shoulders.

'As I said just now, Carrie, it's too lovely an evening not to make the best of it. I'd like to show you the lake.'

And put like that, how could Carrie refuse?

6

'You could wear this,' Morgan said, holding out a buoyancy aid towards Carrie.

'No I couldn't,' Carrie said. 'I don't do water. And I can't come to Cannes with you.'

'Another weekend then?'

Oh dear, he wasn't giving up, was he? Morgan was dangling a buoyancy aid in front of her, and she could see a sales ticket hanging from it.

'But that's new!' Carrie said. 'There's still a price tag on it.'

'I know. I had a job finding it in Grangeleigh, I can tell you. I could have bought any number of things with which to shear sheep or milk cows or feed chickens, but a buoyancy aid eluded me for hours.'

'But you found one in the end.'

'I did. But I had to guess your size . . . '

Morgan's voice trailed away, his eyes resolutely on Carrie's, but it still made her shiver to think his eyes had been on her — when she wasn't looking probably — trying to judge her size.

'You bought it for me?'

'I did.'

Carrie was touched at his thoughtfulness, yet embarrassed, too, that he'd spent money on her.

'I don't like to think of you wasting your money on me,' Carrie said, gently. After all a gift was a gift, whatever it might be, and Morgan had bought it for her — and no one else.

'It won't be a waste if you wear it. We can take the dinghy on the lake. I've got the trailer hitched to the Land Rover ready.'

Morgan tilted his head to one side, looked at Carrie questioningly — almost pleadingly she thought.

'Now?'

'Why not now? It's perfect for sailing. It will give you a taster for when you *do* come to Cannes.'

'I haven't said I'm coming to Cannes.'

'You'd love it, I promise you. Anyway, in the meantime, I've got an old waterproof you can wear. It's one I had as a teenager — a bit faded and tatty now, but it will do.'

Oh yes, she thought, and I'm going to look so sexy in that — not!

She looked at her watch. She'd promised to call in on her mother later.

'An hour?' Morgan said.

My, but he was keen.

'Three quarters,' Carrie said. 'I've promised my mother I'll call in on my way home. The hire van should be here in time.'

She explained how her mother was anxious about answering the door in the dark, and how she bolted herself in once the streetlamps came on so that even with a key Carrie would be unable to get in.

'It won't be dark for ages yet. And I guarantee you're going to enjoy this,' Morgan said.

He raced off somewhere, coming back with an old windcheater.

'Hold your arms out,' he said, and Carrie duly complied with the demand, as Morgan fed her arms into the bulky sleeves and sealed the wristbands securely. Then he zipped it up for her, as though she was a child needing help. He did it so gently, his hands carefully gliding past the small mounds of her breasts without touching until he clicked the popper shut at the neck. 'And now the buoyancy aid. I'll need to pull tighter with that. Okay?'

'Okay,' Carrie said as he helped ease her into it as he had with the windcheater.

'You look great,' Morgan said.

I do? I feel like a trussed up chicken, actually, was what she wanted to say. But even though she was anxious about being in a tiny dinghy she was excited too. She'd always had an adventurous spirit — and it had been Aaron who'd knocked it out of her, she realised now.

'I'll try not to be sick,' Carrie said with a grin.

* * *

'What do I have to do?' Carrie asked, as Morgan helped her into the dinghy. How small her hand was in his, how warm and dry his hand was, and how safe she felt.

'Sit there for a moment until I cast off. Then you'll have to keep out of the way of the boom. I'll need to go about quickly if we're not to hit the bank over there.'

'I hope not,' Carrie said. 'I can't swim, remember.'

'I remembered. Hence the buoyancy aid.'

'Right,' Carrie said.

'I won't confuse you with science right now, but you will need to move quickly from port to starboard when I tell you.'

'Um . . .'

'You don't know which is which?'

'Port's left, but which is left on a boat?' Carrie asked as Morgan raised the sails, secured the ropes.

'Don't worry about it. I'll point. Okay? But we'll need to move now because the breeze is filling the sail.'

The dinghy wobbled and Carrie clutched the side. Morgan pushed off from the bank and suddenly it was just them and the breeze and the lowering sun and a bird singing somewhere high in a tree. For half an hour it was just them, and Carrie could forget about Morgan having a woman somewhere he wanted to have children with.

'Like it?' Morgan asked. 'Hang on tight! I'm going to go about now.'

'It's nothing like the cross channel ferry,' Carrie laughed as they returned to an even keel. 'I don't feel the teensiest bit sick. Yet!'

'Ah,' Morgan said. 'That could all change. Because in that basket there is some champagne. And glasses. And just so we don't drink on an empty stomach I've brought some canapés from the deli in the village. Right, head down, I'm dropping the sail now.'

Morgan guided the dinghy to the bank and tied up. Then he opened the half bottle of champagne and handed the glasses to Carrie, their hands touching and in the instant they did, their eyes met and held. Carrie couldn't help noticing that Morgan's hands shook as he pulled the cork — the pop loud in the stillness of the late afternoon. There was a plop as the cork landed in the lake, and Carrie laughed.

'Only one glass, then,' she said.

'Me too. My plane goes at dawn.'

'That early?'

'That early,' Morgan said.

And the air seemed to be charged between them. There was nothing but silence because now even the birds had stopped singing. Carrie could feel the thump of her heart against her ribs — the effect of being so close to Morgan.

'Shall I open this?' Carrie asked,

breaking the silence, pointing to the box of canapés.

'Please. Then come and sit here or we might topple over.' He patted the seat beside him in the stern, just wide enough for two. Carrie slid along the seat until you couldn't have got a hair between her thigh and Morgan's, but they didn't touch. She didn't dare.

★   ★   ★

'Mmm, but those were so good,' Carrie said, finishing a third smoked salmon blini. She'd already eaten two bite-sized wild mushroom vol-au-vents and a vegetable samosa.

'Glad you like them,' Morgan said, smiling.

'All this fresh air's given me an appetite. I can't believe how peaceful it is here,' Carrie said.

'This was my sanctuary when I was a boy,' Morgan said. 'The place I always ran to in times of trouble.'

'Are you running now?' Carrie asked,

turning to look thoughtfully at him.

'From?'

'Anything. Anyone.'

Morgan put down his glass and placed his hands either side of Carrie's face and tilted her head to his. She didn't resist, but she knew her eyes were wide with shock — she could see herself reflected in Morgan's pupils.

Then Morgan touched his lips to the tip of her nose. He seemed to be waiting for her to respond, for her to push him away, or remonstrate — but she didn't. She couldn't.

'Only from myself,' Morgan said.

Then he brushed his lips against hers, just a feathery kiss, and she closed her eyes.

'I've been wanting to do that since the moment I met you,' Morgan said. His hands still held Carrie's face, and her eyes were still closed. Slowly she opened them, but didn't speak. And she didn't move. 'Come to Cannes with me, Carrie, please?'

'I can't,' she said. 'I've already told

you I can't do weekends.'

She reached up to place her hands on Morgan's and pulled them away from her face, but she did it gently.

'Can't or won't?'

'Can't.'

'Why not?'

'I'd rather not go into that.'

'But you're not cross I kissed you?'

'I'd rather not answer that.'

'Ah,' Morgan said, as Carrie felt colour tinge her cheeks. 'Then, I think you enjoyed that kiss every bit as much as I did.'

'It was hardly a kiss,' she said.

'Well, I can soon rectify that!' Morgan laughed, but Carrie put up a hand to stop him.

'No! I can't deny I didn't enjoy it because it's been a long time since anyone has kissed me — or wanted to kiss me — but I don't think it's right. You're my employer and I think it is going to be best for us both if we keep it that way.'

Carrie scrambled to her feet and

went to the side of the dinghy. She yanked on the mooring rope until the side touched the bank of the lake. Then she swung one leg over onto the shore, and then the other until she was standing on the grass glaring down at Morgan.

'And we've both got responsibilities!' she yelled at him, before turning towards the track that went towards the house. 'Haven't we? You to whoever it is you have asked me to decorate the nursery for, and — '

'I can explain, if — ' Morgan called after her.

'Forget it, Morgan. I'll see you on Monday. Have a good weekend.'

As Carrie ran down the track, she prayed her hire van would be waiting in the drive.

* * *

Carrie got caught in a queue of traffic going into Farchester — a queue so slow that at times she'd killed the engine and simply waited for traffic to start again. The queue had only just got going again, but was creeping along — a snail could have moved faster.

Her lips were still tingling from Morgan's kiss, as soft and as unthreatening as it had been. How could he? He was planning a nursery for his future family with his future wife and he'd kissed her — Carrie. And he'd got her out on the water under the pretext of having bought her a buoyancy aid especially so that she'd feel obliged to go, hadn't he?

And then there'd been that moment when she'd opened her eyes after the kiss and all she'd wanted to do was put her arms around his neck, pull him to her, kiss him long and hard and feel him kiss her back. It had all been so perfect out there on the lake. The sun had hovered a long time in the sky, turning it a pearly pink, then crimson, before sinking.

Well, just forget him, Carrie Fraser, she told herself as she parked in her mother's drive. It will just be another Friday evening for you while Mum decides what she wants to eat for supper on Saturday and for Sunday lunch. And then you'll go to the supermarket on the way back to your flat and buy the groceries.

But something didn't feel right as at last she arrived in her mother's road. Her mother's bungalow was in darkness. The hall light should have been on, but wasn't. The curtains should have been drawn to shut out the night, but weren't.

Carrie yanked on the handbrake and got out of the hire van. She slammed the door shut before running to the front door and ringing the bell. There was no response. Something was seriously wrong here, Carrie knew it.

Racing around to the back of the bungalow, Carrie found the spare — hopefully burglar-proof — key at the bottom of the garden under the watering can and raced back again, letting herself in through the kitchen.

'Mum! It's only me!' Carrie called into the darkness, her voice a wobble of fear that she might find her mother collapsed somewhere. She snapped on the kitchen light. No dishes were on the side waiting for her to wash up as there often were if her mum knew she was calling.

After a rapid search of the bungalow, her breathing coming fast and shallow, it soon became obvious that her mother wasn't around. Her wheelchair was parked and folded, as it always was when not in use, in the small hallway.

The place felt cold — as if no one had been in it for a while. Racing back to the kitchen, Carrie put her hand to the kettle — stone cold.

Might there be a note for her somewhere, telling her where her mother had gone? Carrie tried all the obvious places but found nothing. If only she'd been able to persuade her mother to use a mobile phone then she could have rung that, but her mother had always argued that there would be no point, she never went anywhere these days.

Well she had now — but where, and with whom?

Carrie took several deep breaths to calm herself. There were no obvious signs that her mother had struggled with anyone, or that anyone had broken in, so Carrie decided to wait for half an hour before taking any further action. Her mother couldn't have gone far unaided, that was for certain — and whoever she was with would soon bring her back, wouldn't they?

But the minutes ticked by slowly, so slowly. When the half hour was up, Carrie rang her mother's neighbours, but no one knew where she was. One of them said they'd seen the man deliver her lunch as normal.

Carrie sat at the kitchen table and watched the minute hand tick another five minutes slowly around the clock. Should she try the hospital to see if her mother had been admitted? Or the police? Yes, hospital first.

Carrie had just dialled the second number for the hospital when her mobile beeped.

Immediately she stopped dialling to answer it.

'Mum?' she said.

'Er, no, Carrie. It's me — Morgan.'

Morgan? Why him? Why now? Carrie could feel her heart rate increase and it was already going fast enough with worry over her mother. A wave of relief rippled through her that she wasn't so alone if Morgan was on the end of the phone. She tried to find her voice to ask Morgan why he was ringing, but couldn't.

'Carrie? Are you okay? Where are you?'

'I'm at my mother's but . . . but . . . she's not here.' Carrie's voice began to break.

'But you were expecting her to be?'

'Yes. I told you. But it's not like her not to be here. I'm . . . '

'Right,' Morgan said. 'I can tell you're worried. Give me your mother's

112

full name, age and address and I'll do some ringing around.'

'You mean hospitals and the police,' Carrie said, her voice small and to her own ears sounding a long way off. 'I was just going to do . . . '

'Name, age, address, Carrie.'

Carrie gave him the information.

'Okay. Now sit tight. Try not to worry too much. There's sure to be some very logical reason why she isn't there. I'll be with you in, say, forty minutes.'

'But . . . ' Carrie began, but Morgan had already hung up.

Morgan had an early start in the morning if he was to get to the airport in time for his flight, didn't he? She wondered why he had called her anyway — to try and persuade her to go with him no doubt. But whatever the reason, she was glad he had — she felt bolstered by his taking charge of the situation.

Slowly, Carrie rose from her chair — all her hard physical work over the past few days and now this emotional worry was making her ache, as though she was going down with something.

She went to the hall window and peered outside. There was nothing but darkness. And then she saw a car's headlights beam around the corner of the close. Carrie pressed her nose against the glass to see better. Not her mother — Morgan. She yanked open the front door to let him in.

'Any news from the police or the hospital?' she asked.

'None.' Morgan put an arm around her shoulder and steered her down the hall towards the lighted kitchen and a chair. 'Sit down. I'm going to make you a cup of tea. Strong, not much milk, no sugar. Right?'

'Right,' Carrie said, and despite the worrying situation she was in, she couldn't help smiling at the thought Morgan had remembered such a small, personal, domestic detail.

'And something to eat. My guess is my little canapés were the last thing you've eaten today.'

'Yes,' Carrie said. 'And that wasn't very long ago. I'm not so weak I can't make a cup of tea.'

'But you aren't going to. I am.' Morgan pressed her further into the chair, then went to the fridge and found cheese and butter and some bread. Within seconds he had a rough and ready sandwich prepared. 'Now eat.'

Carrie nibbled daintily at the sandwich, not really having the appetite for it but Morgan had been kindness itself in making it for her. It occurred to her how different her mother's small bungalow was compared to Morgan's beautiful house. How different their lives were — not that it seemed to be bothering Morgan at the moment.

'Tell me about your mother,' he said. 'While we wait.'

So, as the minutes continued to tick around the clock and there was still no sign of Louise, Carrie talked. She told him about her mother being widowed so young, and how she'd had to work so hard to keep a roof over their heads.

And about her father's gambling which had left them so poor.

'He earned a good salary as a doctor — in both public and private practice — but it meant, in the end, that he had more to fritter away,' Carrie finished.

'So, I'm not the only one with a gambler in the family,' Morgan said.

'You too?'

'My brother.'

'It's tough, isn't it?' Carrie said, and Morgan nodded. 'It's an addiction. Not an addiction like alcohol and cigarettes that eventually shows in your face, but an *invisible* addiction. An illness, I suppose.'

Carrie had been sent on a counselling course by her doctor — not long after her father's death to try and understand what it was that had made him gamble, but she doubted she ever would.

'But a bloody expensive one!' Morgan said — anger at how his brother's gambling had affected him in his voice.

'Yes. I was taken out the private

school I was at when Dad could no longer pay the fees. I went to the local comp. Gambling killed my father in the end. It was an open verdict, but . . . well, I don't have to say it, do I?'

There — it was out in the open. Or almost. Suicide. She hadn't been able to talk about it before, but with Morgan and his shared experience of having a gambler in the family, it seemed easier somehow.

Morgan slid his chair along the floor until he was close to Carrie. He put his arms around her, pulling her head down onto his shoulder.

'Gambling killed my brother in the end, too — too much time spent in casinos drinking too much brandy. He was well over the limit the night he and Georgina crashed the car.'

Carrie saw him glance at the kitchen clock and then quickly away again. Were they both thinking the same thing — that somehow it had all got too much for Louise and . . . no, Carrie wasn't even going to think it.

'I'll ring those numbers again,' Morgan said, going to the phone in the hall.

He came back shaking his head — no one called Louise Fraser had been admitted anywhere.

'You'd better go,' Carrie said. 'You've got an early flight.'

'It'll wait,' he said.

'Flights don't wait, Morgan.'

Carrie hurried to the window and peered out, but there was still no sign of her mother.

'No, no,' Morgan said. 'Of course they don't.'

'Then go. Thanks for helping — I really appreciate it. But you haven't said why you rang. Why did you?'

'Come away from the window and I'll tell you — you aren't going to make Louise suddenly materialise by staring out into the dark.'

'I know,' Carrie said. Morgan was holding his hand out towards her.

'Come on. Come here.'

Carrie slipped her hand into his and let herself be led from the window.

'I only rang to thank you for coming out in the dinghy with me,' Morgan said. 'And to say I hope you'd have a good weekend, whatever it was you were going to do.'

'But now it's not good,' Carrie said.

'So, I'll wait until it gets better,' Morgan said. He pulled Carrie to him, and kissed her gently on the lips — another feathery kiss, almost platonic, yet it was the sort of kiss Carrie needed right at that moment. She put her arms around his neck and pulled herself closer to him, needing his comfort, needing his caring.

And that's how her mother found them when she opened the back door.

'Carrie!'

'Mum!'

It was hard to say who had the bigger surprise — Louise to find her daughter in a man's arms when she'd been pretty certain Carrie hadn't been seeing anyone, or Carrie to see a man she'd not seen before holding her mother's hand and gazing adoringly at her.

7

'Mum, he was holding your hand!' Carrie said.

'Well, of course he was, darling,' Louise said. 'He was helping me up the path.'

'From where?' Carrie asked.

'A concert. At St. Andrew's. To raise funds for a public sculpture.'

'And you didn't think to leave me a note?'

'Well, I did think about it, and I started writing one, but then I thought I'd have been back before you arrived . . . ' Louise's voice trailed away and she smiled to herself.

'But you weren't?'

Carrie struggled to keep jealousy that her mother had obviously had a better time than she had out of her voice.

'No. There was coffee in the chancel so we stopped for that. Then Paul suggested a glass of wine on the way back. You know how these things happen.'

Again that little smile to herself and Carrie thought, well, things might have happened like that for me once, but not for quite some time. And to think she'd turned down a trip to Cannes with Morgan!

'And you completely forgot I'd said I'd call in?'

'Yes . . . I mean no, I didn't forget exactly. But everything was all rather last minute. Paul brought me my lunch as usual and I happened to have Mozart on the radio, and he mentioned the concert on this evening. We had an interesting conversation about Mozart and then he asked if I'd like to go to the concert. So I did. I took longer than I thought I would to get ready — you know a shower and changing my clothes and everything. But it was all worth it because the concert was rather good actually.'

'And you didn't take your chair. You

never go anywhere without it normally.'

'I know. But it wasn't far from the car park. Paul said he'd help.'

'But you hardly know him!'

'I could say the same of you and the man you had your arms wrapped around!'

'I was worried, Mum,' Carrie said. 'Morgan rang the hospital and the police for me — twice. He was just being kind.'

'Hmm,' Louise said. 'The way he was looking at you . . . '

'Was probably much the way Paul was looking at *you*!'

'Darling, let's not argue,' Louise said.

'I'm not arguing,' Carrie said. 'I'm glad you've had such a lovely time, but you gave me a scare.'

'I know that now. And I'm sorry,' Louise said. 'Cup of tea?'

'Not for me, thanks,' Carrie said. 'Morgan made me so many cups of tea I'm in danger of drowning in it. Tell me what you want to eat for the weekend and then I'll go.'

'Ah . . . ' Louise said. She fiddled with the silk scarf at her neck, loosening the knot, then tightening it again.

'Ah what, Mum?'

'Um . . . Paul's taking me bird-watching tomorrow. We're going to take a picnic.'

'Bird-watching?'

'Yes. Along the canal. In my wheel-chair in case you're worried I have to stand around too long. And then on Sunday he's invited me to lunch at the Turf Lock Inn. So — '

'So I'm pensioned off?' Carrie interrupted.

'I thought you'd be glad to be released from your duty for a while.'

'It's not a *duty*, Mum! I do it because I want to, you know, for all you did for me when Dad died and because of your arthritis.'

Carrie felt her emotions welling up again. It had been a worry wondering where Louise was. And Morgan turning up and being so kind had touched her. And he'd kissed her again — another platonic kiss, but in the circumstances it was all she had needed. She wondered just what his kisses might be like if he were to let his emotions run away with him.

'I know, darling, I know,' Louise said. 'You've been more than wonderful to me — I couldn't have wished for a better daughter. And, perhaps, I've rather taken advantage of that. But now . . . well, now maybe it's time we both moved on a little? Perhaps you could see Morgan this weekend.'

'No can do. He's flying to Cannes in the morning.'

'Ah, but you'd like to go with him?'

'I didn't say that.'

'You didn't have to. But he has asked you, yes?'

'Yes,' Carrie said.

'Well ring him and tell him you're free to go now, darling. You've been on your own far too long.'

'You sound as though you're trying to get rid of me!' Carrie looked mock-outraged. And then another thought occurred to her — might Louise want Paul to stop the night? Her mother was barely sixty, for goodness' sake — still young enough to have sex if she wanted to . . . in fact for all Carrie knew, that was exactly what she was having every weekday when Paul brought lunch. The thought made her feel distinctly uncomfortable. Jealousy, she reminded herself, is not a healthy attribute to have.

And then another thought occurred to Carrie — if she did ring Morgan and he could get her on the same flight, might the fact she was looking so keen mean he would expect sex with her as a given?

'The phone, Carrie?' Louise said, smiling at her.

Carrie shrugged.

'I don't know that it would be a good idea.'

'You can't let one bad apple put you off apples for life, darling,' Louise said.

Her eyes were glittering with happiness, Carrie noticed. Just what, she wondered, had occurred between Paul and her mother, and when and where, and how often? And why hadn't she noticed before?

Carrie shrugged again, but said nothing. What could she say? What is sex like with a new man after so long a time without, Mum? No, she could hardly say that. And yet it was what she most wanted to know.

'Phone him, Carrie.'

'When I get back to my flat,' Carrie said, gathering up her jacket and her bag. 'Maybe.'

⋆ ⋆ ⋆

Back at her flat, Carrie searched drawers looking for her passport — if she could find it she *would* ring Morgan and ask if she could join him after all. It would be good to see Gen again, and meet Jean-Claude. She regretted the years she'd wasted letting their friendship drift to birthday and Christmas cards and the occasional

126

e-mail. She knew, in her heart of hearts, it was Gen who had kept the friendship alive more than she had. And she had so much to thank her friend for in getting her the commission for Oakenbury Hall.

Damn, where was the thing?

Then a thought struck her — what was the likelihood of getting on the same flight as Morgan even if she did find it? Probably nil. And if she couldn't, would she get one in time to make going all that way worthwhile?

Decisions, decisions. But there had been something about the look of pure happiness on her mother's face that someone — in this case Paul — cared for her, and cared enough to cope with her handicap, that had Carrie scrolling through her phone book for Morgan's number. Carrie wanted that pure happiness for herself — life couldn't be all work, as it had been up to now. Her passport had to be here somewhere — she'd carry on looking until she found it.

Even if she couldn't find happiness with Morgan, at least if she went to Cannes she might find out who the mysterious woman he was wanting to have babies with was. And then she could get him out of her life — move on and seek that happiness elsewhere.

But every time Carrie pressed 'call' all she got was Morgan's answerphone service on his mobile. And when she rang the landline the engaged tone purred in her ear every time.

Ah well. Carrie shrugged. Obviously a trip to Cannes wasn't meant to be.

★　★　★

Carrie didn't sleep well. She dozed off at last just as it was getting light again. And then she was jerked into wakefulness by a knock at the door.

'Who on earth . . . ?'

Carrie stumbled from bed, grabbed a robe and slipped into it, pulling it around her without bothering to fasten it properly. She'd see who it was and then get back to sleep.

Putting the security chain on, Carrie opened the door.

The postman stood there grinning at her. She pulled her robe more tightly round her but realised she'd have to take the security chain off and open the door to take in the large package being held out towards her.

'Thanks,' she said, taking the package. It was the fabric samples and trimmings she'd sent for, to add to her work book to show potential clients. There might be something inside suitable for Morgan's nursery. Apple green perhaps.

And then she saw the car, parked by the kerb at the end of her garden path. A sleek, low, sports car. Vintage. Now who would own a wonderful car like that around here? she wondered.

Someone was sitting in the driver's seat, head bent low over the steering wheel. As though whoever it was had dozed off. Longish fair hair that curled down the side of the neck. Male.

Morgan. Oh my God, what was he doing here?

Clutching the package, Carrie walked, barefoot, down her garden path. She opened the gate slowly, and for once it didn't squeak. Was Morgan all right? He hadn't noticed her walking towards him. Perhaps he'd been there all night and was asleep?

Tentatively, Carrie tapped the glass.

Morgan jerked awake, leaping in his seat so that this head hit the roof lining of the low-slung car.

'What are you doing here?' Carrie said.

Morgan frowned — obviously he hadn't been able to hear her through the glass and couldn't lip-read. He wound the window down — a hand lever Carrie noticed.

Carrie bent down so that her head was level with his.

'What are you doing here?'

'Er, missed my flight,' he said.

'And you've been here ever since waiting for me to get up?'

'Something like that,' Morgan said.

'Oh God, and it's all my *fault!*' she said. 'All that fuss over my mother and she was out on a date, for heaven's sake.'

'Looked like she'd had a good time,' Morgan said.

'Better than we did,' Carrie replied. 'Well, apart from, you know, when you comforted me and, um . . . '

'Kissed you?'

Carrie pressed her lips together and nodded. She so wanted to kiss him again, but as she was only partly dressed, and outside on the pavement in view of the neighbours should they be up and peering out of their windows, she thought she'd better not.

'I was happy to help,' Morgan said. 'With or without the kiss.'

'But now you've missed your flight. I'm sorry. I'd ask you in but . . . '

'You've got someone there?'

Carrie thought he looked really upset that this might be the case.

'No . . . it's just that, well, I'm not

131

the tidiest of people on my home patch. I'm not a very good ambassador for my trade, I'm afraid.'

'I won't look,' Morgan said. 'If you'll just stand back, I'll get out. Legs are a bit stiff.'

'Follow me,' Carrie said, doing as she was told.

She ran back up her path.

Once inside, Carrie raced around like a headless chicken plumping up cushions, clearing magazines and newspapers and fabric samples off the couch so Morgan could sit down. He seemed so large in her tiny flat. So very out of place. But what else could she have done really but ask him in, seeing as it was her fault he'd missed his flight?

'I'll put the kettle on and then get changed,' Carrie said, pulling her robe tightly around her. Oh my God, had it been gaping that much all the time she'd been talking to him, bent down on the pavement by his car?

'No rush,' Morgan said, grinning at her.

Just for a moment Carrie allowed herself to imagine who it might be Morgan was thinking of having babies with, but then told herself firmly that it was time she put herself first for a change. And Morgan was here with her and not with whatever-her-name-was, wasn't he? His choice. Or was it? Was he here only because he'd missed his flight?

And then she fled to the bathroom, showered rapidly and towelled herself roughly, before dressing in jeans and a black and white polka-dot blouse.

Carrie ran down the hall towards her sitting room, running a brush through her hair as she went. Then the smell of strong coffee hit her. Carrie pivoted around and back towards the kitchen.

'Pardon me for taking liberties, but I thought I'd make a start on coffee.' Morgan beamed at her. 'I know how long it takes a woman to get ready.'

'I'm sure you do,' Carrie snapped.

She didn't want to know how many women Morgan might have woken up with, might have made coffee for — not right now she didn't; all she wanted to do at that moment was take Morgan back to bed with her for some nice, long slow love-making. And then she remembered she was right out of the habit of love-making and would probably move at the wrong time and come across as a spinster of long-standing.

'Not that you've taken very long.'

'I never do,' Carrie said. 'And, trust me, the mother of your children won't take very long either once your nursery is fully functional. Although I expect you'll be having a nanny.'

Best remind him of that right now before she did something — like slide her arms around his neck and kiss him long and slow and deep.

'That,' Morgan said, taking two mugs down from their hooks under Carrie's one and only pair of wall cupboards, 'will depend on what the mother of my children wants. Now then, if you point me in the direction of the bread bin, I'll make toast.'

'Oh, but you don't have to. I can do that.'

'Oh, but I will. It's the least I can do for inviting myself in and making you rush when I'm sure that was the last thing you wanted to do. I hope I'm not keeping you from anything today? You know, responsibilities?'

'My mother,' Carrie said, 'seems to have absolved me of them with someone called Paul.'

'Ah. In that case, after we've had breakfast, perhaps you could throw a few things in a bag and we'll catch that flight after all?'

Oh yes, please, Carrie thought. Then I'll be able to quiz Gen or generally just keep my eyes and ears open to find out who this mysterious potential mother of Morgan's children is and get him out of my system once and for all.

'Um . . . ' Carrie said.

'You haven't got any excuses left, Carrie,' Morgan said, his face serious. He'd found the bread bin all on his own and was cutting great doorsteps for toast.

'Oh yes, I have,' Carrie said. 'I can't find my passport.'

'I'll help you find it,' Morgan said. 'Is there anywhere you haven't looked?' He glanced around the room and grinned. 'You seem to have been pretty thorough in your searching.'

'I was. There's only the top airing cupboard left and I can't reach that. Not without a set of steps, and those are strapped to the roof of my hired van.'

'Point me to it, then,' Morgan said.

'Even if we find it,' Carrie said, 'I don't know that it's a good idea for me to come with you.'

She made no move to show him where the airing cupboard was. Instead she put two more slices of bread in the toaster and depressed the button.

'Well, *I* do. Genifer would love to see you.'

'That's blackmail.'

'Incentive.'

'Top of the stairs, on the left,' Carrie said.

If he were to find her passport there,

then she'd go with him. Maybe.

But it was more than her passport that Morgan found. He came into the kitchen carrying her tatty case — the only one she had because Aaron had taken the new ones they'd bought for their honeymoon.

Instantly, Carrie remembered what was in the case. Her wedding dress. And shoes. And trousseau — such a wonderfully old-fashioned word, trousseau.

And her engagement ring — sapphires the same shade of blue as her eyes — in a black velvet box.

'This is all that was in there,' Morgan said. 'I opened it, but closed it again when I realised what it contained.'

But he hadn't shut it properly and there was a crushed piece of raw slub silk hanging out the side.

'Oh. Oh, I'd forgotten . . . '

And then Carrie burst into tears, her sobs making her shoulders judder, and her breathing jagged.

'Ssh, ssh, it's all right. We all hang

onto things for all sorts of reasons, when sometimes perhaps we shouldn't.'

He was still clutching the suitcase to him.

'Do we?' Carrie sniffed.

'I've still got a photograph of Georgina. Just the one. But it's time for it to go, I think.' Morgan placed the suitcase very carefully on the table and opened his arms to Carrie. 'Come here, sweetheart. Let it all out. I don't suppose you have, have you?'

Carrie shook her head. But she didn't walk into Morgan's outstretched arms. She wanted to walk into them because he wanted to love her and not because he pitied her.

'I'm going to make an executive decision,' Morgan said.

He walked to Carrie and placed a hand behind her head and pulled her gently towards his shoulder.

He began to rock her gently, and she gave herself up to the rhythm of his rocking — her sobs becoming less juddery, quieter.

After what seemed ages, Carrie pulled away from him gently.

'I don't usually weep all over men I've only just met. Sorry. Or even ones I've known for ages actually. And I know I should have thrown it all away long before now,' she said. 'He's not coming back, is he?'

'I think you know the answer to that, Carrie.'

'We could,' Carrie said, 'drop them off at the charity shop on the way to the airport?'

'We certainly could!' Morgan said.

'All except the ring, perhaps,' Carrie said.

'If that's what you want.'

'I do. I'll take that to the jewellers and see if I can sell it,' she said. 'I think the time's come to move on.'

'We'd better shift, then,' Morgan said. 'I'll have to ring the pilot.'

'The pilot? You know the pilot?'

'Well, it *is* my plane,' he said.

8

'Carrie!' Genifer squealed with delight at seeing her — the pleasure and love in her friend's eyes bringing a lump to Carrie's throat. 'This is some surprise!'

'Not least to me!' Carrie laughed.

She gave Genifer a quick resume of what had happened back in Farchester to make her suddenly agree to come over, stealing her gaze away from her friend's face now and then to glance around Morgan's office. It was huge — almost the size of the aircraft hanger the Lear jet had been towed out from. On the walls were poster-sized black and white photos of racing yachts. And portrait shots of lots of celebrities Carrie had only ever seen in magazines or on TV before.

'And thank goodness my passport was in that tatty old case after all,' Carrie finished. She pointed to the celebrity photos. 'Does Morgan know all these people?'

'I wouldn't say he was bestest buddies or anything, but it's quite a gallery, isn't it?' Genifer said. 'All signed with thanks to Morgan. All the aristos . . . '

'Aristos?'

'Well, you do know . . . ' Genifer began, then stopped abruptly. She started tidying papers that didn't really need tidying on the desk.

'Know what, Gen?' Carrie asked.

'Oh, *things*,' Genifer said.

'What sort of things?' Carrie felt a nervous flutter in her stomach, and her mouth went dry. What else didn't she know about Morgan?

'Things I can't tell you, Carrie. Sorry. Now, everything's up to date here, so shall we go hit Monaco and some shops?'

'I don't think so,' Carrie said. 'One, I haven't brought any euros with me, and two, I really can't afford to buy things I don't need. And I've . . . '

'Stop!' Genifer held up a hand. She reached in the drawer of the desk and pulled out a wad of notes. She waggled them at Carrie. 'Morgan's left this little lot. Spending money.'

'Well, you can leave it there,' Carrie said. She didn't want Morgan spending his money on her, because she didn't want to feel obliged. Or have him feel sorry for her that she was strapped for cash. 'Where is Morgan anyway?'

'Gone to his villa. Things he needed to do, he said. Now, are you sure you won't change your mind about spending this little lot?'

'Certain.'

'Okay. Well, we'll go to Monaco anyway. At least let me buy you a coffee. And I'll treat you to lunch.'

'You're on,' Carrie said. It really was good to see Gen — see her looking so well, and so pleased to see her. Just for a second, Carrie wondered if Gen had had to cancel anything at short notice to spend time with her. But she decided not to ask. 'Hey,' she said instead, 'you've really settled into the life down here — driving on the other side of the road and all that!'

'Oh, we're not driving,' Genifer said. 'We're walking over to Quai M. Laubeuf and the helicopter. Morgan's orders.'

★   ★   ★

'The famed Casino,' Genifer said, waving an arm towards the grand steps up which two women Carrie vaguely recognised were running on very high heels. 'Monte Carlo in a nutshell.'

'I've only ever seen it in films,' Carrie said. 'It's smaller than I thought it was, and yet more grand. Does that make sense?'

'Perfect sense,' Genifer said.

'And is that Merriel, um, what's her name, just going inside? And that other one . . .'

'Merriel Evans. And Johanna Beaumont. They live together here somewhere.'

'You mean as in lovers?'

'I expect so,' Genifer laughed. 'Gosh, you really do live a sheltered life back in Farchester if the very idea of a couple of women living together throws you like that — you should see your face!'

'It doesn't throw me — I just thought, you know, they're always wrapped around some hunk of a bloke in films.'

'And films are fantasy, right?' Genifer said.

Carrie felt herself blush. She must be coming across as so unworldly, so gauche. Was that how Morgan saw her?

'Sorry, sweetheart,' Genifer said, 'I didn't mean to upset you. But you're going to have to get used to seeing celebrities in Monaco — they're all over the place. And in Cannes. When you live here you see it all as normal. And you learn to be very discreet about who is seen with whom and where and how many times. Especially who hires Morgan's yachts and what they get up to on them.'

'You do?'

'And so will you when you've been here a few more times — Morgan expects it of his employees. Morgan *has* mentioned he wants a complete make-over at his villa, and he'd like you to do it, hasn't he?'

Which, Carrie thought, was a not very subtle reminder that was exactly what she was — just one of Morgan's employees, nothing special. And this was the first she'd heard about being commissioned to do a makeover on Morgan's villa. But she nodded, not knowing what to say.

But it seemed that Genifer hadn't noticed her gaffe. She steered Carrie to an outside table of the Café de Paris. They sat down, Carrie feeling like a kid in a toyshop looking at all the expensive goodies — clothes and bags and shoes — on display. Women's chatter — like birds joyfully greeting a new dawn — filled the air. But, Carrie noticed, while they might have drunk their coffee, their cakes remained uneaten on the plates.

Within seconds a waiter glided up

and took their order, and Carrie was surprised to hear her friend speaking rapidly in French — far too fast for her to translate from her ill-remembered school day French lessons.

'I've ordered coffee and *galettes aux pignons* — sort of pine nut biscuity things. Okay?'

'Fine,' Carrie said. 'And your French is impressive!'

'I should hope so,' Genifer said. 'The length of time I've been here! Yours will be, too, the longer you're here.'

Carrie shrugged.

'I don't know that I'll be here long.'

'Well, unless you're Wonder Woman and can whiz through the makeover of Morgan's villa, it's going to take you a while.'

'That's something I'll need to discuss with Morgan,' Carrie said, perhaps a bit too sharply.

'Oooh, have I touched a raw nerve? You know, Aaron . . . '

'Who? Who?' Carrie said, a faux-puzzled look on her face.

Genifer reached across the table and hugged her friend, and Carrie hugged her back.

'Sorry,' she said.

'Forgiven,' Carrie told her.

'Now, are you sure you don't want so spend some of that money Morgan left for you?'

'Absolutely certain,' Carrie said. 'Although, I suppose I could buy a pretty scarf or something for my mother.'

'Of course you can. We'll have lunch over by the Grimaldi palace — the pink walls of the buildings over there look so pretty in the afternoon sun. And we'll shop on the way. Okay?'

'Okay.'

The two women fell silent — Genifer eating her galette and Carrie people-watching. There were so many beautiful people here, so much wealth being paraded in clothes and shoes and handbags.

A Rolls Royce purred to a halt outside the Casino, and a uniformed member of staff appeared as if by magic, to open the driver's door. British number plates, she noticed. A tall, elegantly dressed man got out and without speaking handed over his keys.

'But that's . . . that's . . . ' Carrie said, but the name of the British MP flew from her mind. 'Oh, I can't think who he is now.'

'Well, best forget anyway,' Genifer laughed. 'And best not notice who that is arriving now.' Genifer pointed to a taxi pulling in where the Rolls Royce had so recently been.

'Oh!' Carrie said, as a well-known UK news announcer slid out of the taxi and hurried up the steps to the Casino. 'I don't think I'll ever get used to this,' she said, thoughtfully, 'you know, all the subterfuge these people must have to go to, to meet whoever it is they ought not to be meeting.'

She shivered remembering how often Aaron had said he was at the gym or working late or visiting his mother, when he wasn't doing any of those things — he was with *her*.

'It's not your worry,' Genifer said. 'And really, it's only a tiny minority. Now, if we're finished here, shall we go?'

★ ★ ★

'In here?' Carrie said. 'We're going in?'

They were standing outside the door of Giorgio Armani.

'Well, we can't let the *vendeuse* know what we want by telepathy, can we?' Genifer laughed, as someone came to open the door for them.

Once inside Carrie stood transfixed — the interior must have cost hundreds of thousands to furnish. Why, the wall lights alone would be in four figures — each.

'Close your mouth,' Genifer giggled. 'You look like a fish gasping for air.'

'Probably,' Carrie said. 'But it's all, sort of, not what I'm used to. Although there are a few interior decorating tips in here I can nick.'

'Ssh, not so loud. Most of these *vendeuses* speak many languages, and can . . . '

' . . . make love in all of them,' Carrie finished for her, sotto voce.

'Oh, you are naughty, but I'm so glad you're here. Now, get shopping!'

★   ★   ★

Carrie allowed Genifer to buy a scarf in sea-green silk for her mother, but refused to let her pay for a kaftan the colour of midnight. It had silver embroidery at the low cut neckline, and Carrie knew it would look perfect with a camisole underneath, worn over her linen trousers.

She'd picked it up and held it against her, and Genifer told her — as she'd known her friend would — that it suited her and why didn't she spend some of Morgan's money on it?

Carrie had said no — it was not a good idea. At the back of her mind, still, was the nursery Morgan had asked her to design for whoever it was that was going to have his children. Was that whom he was with now — unable to wait a second longer to be with her once he'd seen Carrie into Genifer's care? Had he only comforted her the way he had in her flat because he was kind? If people having illicit liaisons was what Morgan was used to, and what he thought of as normal, then it certainly wasn't Carrie's way of doing things.

But then Genifer had spoken to the saleswoman in French far too fast for Carrie to pick out more than a couple of words.

'What did you say?' Carrie had asked, but Genifer had shrugged and said nothing much, just general comments about the colour and the cut and how pretty it was.

Now, after marvelling at the Grimaldi Palace and watching the changing of the guard, and having peered out over the wall to the harbour, full of gin palaces below, Carrie and Genifer were sitting in the shade of the high buildings outside a restaurant.

Carrie picked up a menu and studied it.

'I don't think I'm very hungry,' she said.

'Salade niçoise, then?' Genifer said. 'That's light, and I can ask to have the dressing served separately.'

'It's not that,' Carrie said. 'It's the prices — they're making my eyes water.'

Genifer laughed.

'It *is* steep even by south of France standards,' she said. 'But it will be worth it. Oh, and I've ordered champagne, seeing as I'm not driving.'

Carrie immediately flipped the menu card to see what the prices were for champagne on the back, but Genifer grabbed it from her.

'Relax, Carrie,' she said. 'You're wound tighter than a watch-spring — not that watches have springs these days.'

Carrie laughed nervously. She knew she was tense. And that was because she didn't know what was expected of her. She was beginning to regret coming now. But Morgan had been so kind and understanding when he'd found her wedding dress and all the other things on which she'd once pinned so much hope. It was just his way of giving her a treat, wasn't it? The money angle was irrelevant as far as he was concerned — £10 to Carrie was probably somewhere in the region of £10,000 to Morgan, wasn't it?

'I know,' Carrie said slowly. 'But it all happened so fast this morning. I got the shock of my life to see Morgan sitting outside when I answered the door to the postman. He looked like he'd been there all night.'

'Perhaps he had,' Genifer said. 'I spoke to him just before midnight. But . . . '

'But what?'

'But maybe I've said too much already.'

The waiter arrived then and Genifer gave the order. Seconds later the wine waiter arrived with two glasses and the champagne in a bucket, and he pulled the cork with a faint 'pop'.

'Don't think too much, Carrie,' Genifer said. 'Follow your heart for a change.'

'I did that once, remember? And look what it did to me!'

'That was four years ago. How many men have you slept with since then?'

Carrie laughed — this was so Gen, and they'd slipped back so easily into their old friendship when they could ask the most personal of questions.

'Zero, would you believe?'

'Oh my God!' Genifer said. 'You'll need oiling the first time you have sex now then, won't you?'

'Gen! People will hear!'

Genifer merely shrugged her shoulders and grinned.

'Anyway,' Carrie said, 'I've got Mum to think about.'

'Sure she's not just an excuse for you? You know, you don't have to risk trusting a man again because of your

— in inverted commas — 'responsibili-ties'?'

'Hmm, maybe,' Carrie said. She told Genifer about her mother being missing and about Paul, and how Morgan had come over to help.

'Oh, *that*'s why he rang and cancelled skippering one of our yachts this weekend.'

'He did that?'

'Didn't I just say?' Genifer said. 'By the way, there's a little worry groove in the centre of your forehead.'

Carrie's hand flew to her forehead, but Genifer reached for her hand and pulled it away.

'But being here this weekend should sort that. Try and go with the flow, Carrie. Leave the UK where it is — over there.' Genifer waved an arm in a vague arc. 'Just *be*.'

'I'll try,' Carrie said, sipping carefully so that the bubbles didn't rush up her nose. 'I'm looking forward to us having a good catch-up chat later. You know, the way we did when we were teenagers and I stopped over at your place. We used to stay up all night talking — remember? And we hardly had a wink of sleep.'

'So, where are you going to sleep tonight?' Genifer asked with a saucy wink.

'Well, at your place. Aren't I?'

'Nope,' Genifer said, a slow smile turning up the corners of her mouth. 'Jean-Claude's sister and her three children are filling our place up. You're stopping at the villa with Morgan.'

*   *   *

'Come and look at the view,' Morgan said, rushing out to the terrace to help Carrie from the taxi Genifer had loaded her into. Morgan had already taken her case, it seemed. 'In early spring it's a ribbon of yellow mimosa between here and the sea.'

Normally so self-assured, it seemed to Carrie that Morgan was nervous now as he held out a hand towards her, as though he were anxious she might not take it.

But she did, allowing him to lead her through French doors and across a white marble tiled floor towards the window.

'It's beautiful,' she said, slipping her hand from his. 'There's going to be a lovely sunset, I think.'

'Without a doubt,' Morgan said. 'Oh, and I bought these for you. Sorry they look a bit droopy.'

He picked up a bunch of ranunculus — buttercup-type flowers in deep shades of yellow, orange and red. They were artistically wrapped in purple cellophane with a matching cascade of ribbons. The whole thing looked almost too beautiful to take apart.

'They *do* look like they need water, poor things,' she said. 'Gorgeous colours. Thank you. Lead me to a vase and I'll see if I can revive them.'

'And then a reviving drink for us,' Morgan said. 'I've got champagne chilling.' He picked up the bottle from its bucket of ice, twisted the cork, pulled.

'More champagne?' Carrie said. 'Is that all anyone drinks down here?'

'Or anything else you'd prefer,' Morgan said quickly.

'Champagne will be fine,' Carrie said. 'Seeing as you've already opened the bottle. I'm getting quite a taste for it. But just one glass — I've already had far too much with Gen in Monaco.'

'Good, good. But before you even think it, I'm not trying to get you drunk. I've prepared a room for you.'

'You didn't have to do that. I can go to a hotel and pay with my credit card. You don't have to put me up.'

'But I do, Carrie. I invited you here and I hoped you would accept my hospitality. And besides, it's a working holiday of sorts, because as you can see this room is in dire need of a radical makeover.'

'Just a bit,' Carrie laughed. She was hugging the bouquet, but lifted it away from her body and held it high in the air so that she had both arms to wave about the vastness of the space. 'A room like this could take these deep shades. Which way does the sun come up in the morning?'

'Over the sea. Now, have you brought something to make notes in?' Morgan asked.

All the joy went out of the moment for Carrie — he'd only asked her here to work, hadn't he?

'Yes,' she said. 'Of course.'

*   *   *

'Oh my God!' Carrie gasped.

The flowers having been placed in water, Morgan had shown her to her room, opened the door for her, and then closed it behind her before going back downstairs.

The room was enormous — twice the size of the room they'd been in downstairs.

But it wasn't the room that had made Carrie gasp with surprise. On the bed, laid out beautifully, not a crease or a fold in it, was the kaftan she'd so admired, lusted after even, in Monte Carlo. Suddenly, Carrie was angry — angry with Genifer for going behind her back and buying it.

'Morgan's orders, no doubt!' Carrie snapped the words out and walked towards the bed. Did he think he could buy her by buying her things?

Despite herself, and her deep misgivings about accepting it, she touched the fabric with a finger. Then she ran her hands over the silver embroidery.

It wouldn't hurt to try it on, would it? And if it looked good on her she could always pay Morgan back — whatever it cost. She could work for half a day for nothing if that's what it would take. No, correction — she *would* pay him back by whatever means.

So, after a hot shower in a bathroom that was bigger than Carrie's sitting room back home in Farchester, she took a clean pair of white linen trousers from her case and put them on.

Rummaging about in her case, Carrie realised she'd forgotten to put in a camisole — all she had was a few T-shirts and she couldn't wear any of those underneath. But her best bra, she had put in. And as luck would have it, it was navy blue with just a tiny trace of lace and a few threads of silver embroidery — perfect.

Carrie was struggling to do up the clasp behind her back when there was a knock on the door.

'Dinner in ten minutes, Carrie.'

'Okay. Fine,' she said, feeling any-thing but. She waited until she heard Morgan's footsteps going down the wide wooden staircase to the floor below. Then she pinched herself hard on the back of her hand. 'You really are here, then,' she said, 'and not in the middle of some sort of magazine romance?'

She giggled, the fastening of the bra taking longer than it ever had before.

Then she slid the kaftan down over her body, feeling the fabric caress her almost. It awoke all sorts of feelings in Carrie — the foremost of which was that although she knew she would resist sharing the big bed in this room with Morgan, she had a feeling she might be putty in his expert hands if he were to suggest it.

9

'Wow!' Morgan said as Carrie walked down the stairs towards him.

'I'm going to pay you back,' Carrie said. 'I know this will have been expensive, but I *will* pay you back — I'll work for half a day or whatever to cover the cost.'

'You don't have to, honestly.'

'I want to. I love it so much.'

'Good.'

She'd stopped walking and was now on the first step up, their heads more or less level.

'You've caught the sun,' Morgan said. He made to touch Carrie's cheek but before their skins connected he whipped his hand away.

'Have I?'

'On your cheeks. You've got more freckles than you had when you arrived.'

'Don't remind me!' Carrie said.

'I think they're lovely.'

'You wouldn't if you had them! You should see me in August — I'm more freckles than face.'

'August isn't far away,' Morgan said. 'I can wait. Now come and eat. Outside on the terrace all right for you?'

'Lovely,' Carrie said. She sidestepped around him across the tiles of the hall, the ceramic chill beneath her bare feet. She only had the pair of shoes she'd travelled in and they'd pinched her feet walking up and down the steep hills of Monaco.

'This way, then,' Morgan said. 'Lobster salad to start with. And then there's a lamb couscous warming in the oven. Apricot roulade for dessert.'

'Is that all?' Carrie said laughing.

'And a cheese platter. Plus fruit. Ice cream if you've still got space.'

'Don't tempt me!' she said.

★   ★   ★

'What are your plans?' Morgan asked, as Carrie helped herself to a huge mound of lobster.

'How do you mean?'

'For the future. Now that your mother seems to have got herself a beau.'

'A beau? What a quaint, old-fashioned term! But I don't know that that's what he is. He's been bringing her meals in the week from the hotel I order them from, that's all.'

'Hmm. It looked as though he was doing more for your mother than that from where I was standing!'

'You don't know anything about my mother. It's going to take a special man to take her, and her medical problems, on.'

'Maybe he *is* that man. Give him a chance, Carrie.'

'I didn't say I wasn't,' Carrie said. She grabbed a hunk of baguette and began buttering it thickly, roughly. 'Paul hasn't been around long enough for me to make any sort of judgement yet.'

She swallowed back a glass of champagne barely giving it a chance to touch the sides of her throat. Then she held out the empty glass towards Morgan and he refilled it for her. And she drank that too. Dutch courage.

'Sometimes,' Morgan said, refilling her glass again, 'a man knows in the first second of meeting a woman that she's the one for him.'

'Not you though!' Carrie laughed. 'I saw that newspaper with the 'Love at first sight' article in your waste bin, and you'd written 'Rot!' across it in black felt tip!'

'How do you know it was me?' Morgan asked.

'Got you! You've just fallen into the trap — that last sentence was as much of a confession as I'll ever hear!'

'Well then,' Morgan said, 'women give themselves away at times too.' He reached under the table and brought out a piece of rolled paper. Slipping off the rubber band he smoothed out a drawing. 'Someone, not a million miles from here, drew this.' He waved the drawing at Carrie. 'And I would bet the deeds of this villa that the subject of this drawing is me.'

'Oh my God!' Carrie said. 'Where did you get that?'

'I picked it up off my lawn. *My* lawn. So, I'm safe in saying it's now mine.'

'I must have dropped it. You weren't ssup, sshup, shupposed to find it.'

'I thought not,' Morgan laughed. 'And you're a little drunk.'

'No, I'm not! Can I have it back?'

Carrie held out her hands towards him, but instead of placing her drawing in them, he dropped it on the floor and instead folded his hands around hers.

'No.'

'Yes,' Carrie said, wriggling her hands free. 'It's only a sketch. I was going to do an oil painting of you. For the drawing room in Oakenbury Hall. There ishn't one of you in the house, I noticed, so I thought I'd paint one. As a preshent. For taking me on, sight unsheen, and letting me loose on your home.'

'In that case,' Morgan said, retrieving the drawing from the ground, 'you can have it back. And now couscous, yes? To sober you up?'

'Loads, please,' Carrie said. 'I think I'm going to need it to soak up thish lovely, lovely, champagne.'

★   ★   ★

'I feel . . . shick,' Carrie groaned. She felt like she was floating. And Morgan was very close to her, wasn't he?

'You won't be sick, sweetheart,' he said.

'You're shouting at me.'

'No I'm not. My mouth is close to your ear, that's all.'

'I still think I'm going to be shick.'

'I hope not. I've given you pepper-mint oil.'

'Oil. Oil,' Carrie said. 'Gen says I'll need oiling before sex.'

'Gen said that?'

'Yesh.'

'Why?'

'Becaushe . . . becaushe . . . I am almosht a born-again virgin.'

'You're a bit too drunk for sex right now.'

'I'll have to do it again shome-time . . . '

'And I'm not the man to take advantage of you, the state you're in at the moment.'

'Pleashe.' Carrie made a pouty-kiss shape with her lips. 'Gen says I've got to shtop thinking sho much. I've jusht got to *be*.'

'Very wise words,' Morgan said. 'But perhaps not right at this moment. Now, here we are.'

Carrie felt herself sinking into some-thing soft. She looked around the room, saw her clothes where she'd left them on the floor when she'd changed into the kaftan. She ought to tidy up, but she couldn't move.

'We can't sit here like this all night, Carrie,' Morgan said.

'We'll lie down then,' Carrie said, suddenly throwing herself back on the bed. 'I don't shnore.'

'Oh Carrie,' Morgan groaned. 'I'm not going to . . . '

'Not going to . . . ' Carrie said, quite forgetting what she had intended saying.

'Arms above your head, sweetheart,' Morgan said. 'Can't let you mess up this lovely dress, can we?'

Gently, Morgan eased the kaftan up Carrie's body, slid her arms from the sleeves, and pulled it over her head. Carrie moaned and rolled over onto her stomach.

'You're making this too easy for me, sweetheart,' he said, as he unclipped her bra strap. 'But you'll probably hate yourself for it in the morning. And no doubt me as well. Roll back over, can you?'

'Yesh, shir,' Carrie said, doing as she was told, struggling to sit up at the same time. 'Where are you taking me?'

'You're not going anywhere,' Morgan told her.

Then he kissed the top of her head before laying her gently back down on the bed, and covering her with the duvet.

'Kith me again,' Carrie said.

'No,' Morgan said. 'Not now.'

*   *   *

Carrie finished showering, pulled on the robe she'd found folded neatly on the chair in the bathroom and tiptoed back to the bed. Oh my God! It was still only 7.37 a.m. — so the clock beside the bed told her.

She hoped she hadn't woken Morgan — wherever he was. Then she saw her clothes neatly hanging on the wardrobe door. How had they got there? Had she taken them off — or had Morgan? She'd been naked when she'd woken up, and if truth were told she still felt warm and fuzzy — the way she'd felt last night sitting opposite Morgan on

171

the terrace in the moonlight.

Carrie spun round towards the bed. Was Morgan in there somewhere? And if he was, what might she have let him do to her? Frantically, Carrie patted the mounds of the duvet but there was no one underneath. Then she heard a tap on the door.

'Carrie? Are you okay?'

Morgan came into the room before Carrie could answer. He was carrying a tray with a cafétière of coffee and some croissants — as though he'd known she'd gone for a shower and was now back. And if he knew that then he'd been beside her in the bed all night, hadn't he?

She plonked herself down on the bed as realisation hit her — she'd been drunk out of her mind, Morgan had brought her up to bed, helped her undress, hung up her clothes . . . and probably had sex with her as well, hadn't he?

She pulled the belt of the gown tighter.

'I've seen it all before,' Morgan said.

'That's all right, then. You don't need to see it again,' Carrie said.

God, the sooner she could get out of here and get back to Farchester the better — she should never have come in the first place. Morgan had got her in a weak moment. Well, he wasn't getting her in another one.

'Need and want are two different things, Carrie,' Morgan said.

'Did . . . did . . . ' Carrie began.

'I didn't take advantage of your champagne-induced state if that's what you were going to ask.'

'I didn't think for one moment you would have done, but . . . ' Carrie's eyes strayed to her clothes hanging on the wardrobe. She felt herself burn up with embarrassment remembering she hadn't put any knickers on because they spoiled the line of her linen trousers.

'I've known enough women to know how clothes come off, how bra straps work,' Morgan said. 'So I did what needed to be done. That is a very expensive kaftan, after all.'

'I'll pay you back.'

'You will?' Morgan said, raising an eyebrow.

'For the kaftan I mean. With money. In case you thought I meant something else.'

'Well, last night you did make me a most tantalizing offer.'

'I've just withdrawn it, whatever it was.'

Carrie leapt into the bed, pulled the duvet up high around her neck.

'Oh, Carrie, you are so easy to wind up.'

'Then stop winding me up,' Carrie said. 'I don't usually get drunk and offer myself to men. Oh my God . . . I wasn't sick, was I?'

'No,' Morgan said, 'you weren't. But you fibbed a bit.'

'Fibbed?'

'Fibbed. You said you don't snore. But you do. Very loudly. All night. I've hardly slept a wink.'

Carrie put her face in her hands. This was getting worse and worse.

'Go away,' she said. 'Please.'

How deeply un-sexy was snoring, for goodness' sake?

'Not until you've had some coffee.'

'And then you'll go?'

'It all depends.'

On what, Carrie didn't want to even think about. She held out her hand for the cup of coffee Morgan had now poured. She'd cleaned her teeth but still her mouth felt dry from all the champagne. And, almost unbelievably, given what she thought she'd eaten last night — she had a vague memory of the sensation of sweet apricots and cream on her tongue — she was hungry. So the croissant would go down well.

'We'll get crumbs in the bed,' Carrie said.

'So *we* will,' Morgan said, lifting the duvet on the other side of the bed to Carrie and getting in. 'But it won't matter because my housekeeper will be back later this morning to change the sheets.'

'How much later?' Carrie asked. The memory of Genifer urging her to go with the flow — just be — floated into her mind and refused to float out again. There was a very handsome man getting into the bed beside her right now. He'd already seen her with no clothes on, seen her drunk beyond belief, knew that she snored, yet still he wanted to share her bed.

And he'd been kind enough to make her coffee he knew she needed on the morning after the night before.

'I could always ring and ask her to make it a bit later?'

'Um,' Carrie said, 'I can't make decisions on an empty stomach. Could I have a piece of croissant, please?'

'With pleasure.'

Morgan broke off a piece of croissant and held it towards her lips. But it was a big bit — too big to get into her mouth at once. So Carrie placed her teeth around the croissant and as elegantly as she could — given she was shaking with fright at what her body was telling her she wanted of this man — she bit off a mouthful. But her lips touched Morgan's fingers, and she didn't want to take them away.

So she didn't. Instead she swallowed the morsel of pastry and gently sucked on Morgan's fingers.

'Oh my God, Carrie,' Morgan said, kissing her forehead, then her eyelids, then her nose, before covering her lips with his; his kiss urgent and probing.

His lips then found the side of Carrie's neck and he half kissed, half sucked against her flesh.

'Be gentle with me,' Carrie whispered. 'It's been a long time.'

Then Carrie undid the tie of her robe, and offered herself body and soul to Morgan.

'I want to *be*,' she said as Morgan pulled her robe gently from her. And then, as Morgan began to kiss every single part of her, she gave herself up to his kisses.

Carrie and Morgan were on the terrace just finishing a fresh pot of coffee — the first one he'd made having gone stone cold while they were making love — when Genifer rang and suggested that they all meet up for lunch.

'What do you think?' Morgan asked Carrie, his hand over the mouthpiece. 'Lunch with Genifer and Jean-Claude, or lunch back in bed with me?'

'Ooooh, decisions, decisions,' Carrie giggled. 'But I think it's going to have to be lunch with Gen, don't you?'

Morgan pulled a mock-sorry face.

'Manners dictate we must,' Carrie said, wagging a finger at him. 'Gen gave up a day yesterday to entertain me, so we'll go to lunch.'

'But we'll get away as soon as we can?'

'We will,' Carrie said, smiling at him.

★　★　★

'Come and have the guided tour, Carrie,' Genifer said, as soon as Carrie and Morgan arrived. 'The men will be talking business anyway.'

She linked her arm through Carrie's and pulled her close.

'You should have come over before,' she said. 'I've got friends down here, but it's not the same with them as it was with you.'

'I know,' Carrie said, turning to kiss her friend's cheek. 'I wish I had now.'

'And is that regret anything to do with Morgan? You know, you would have met him sooner, and . . . '

'Don't be silly!' Carrie interrupted.

'Ah, the lady doth protest too much, methinks,' Genifer quipped. 'But I'm not going to give you the third degree.' She opened a door, throwing it wide and ushered Carrie inside. 'Come and look at the view from here.'

'Wow! That's a view and then some,' Carrie said, standing beside Genifer at the window looking out over the harbour at Antibes.

'A view with a purpose!' Genifer laughed. 'Some of Morgan's yachts are moored in Cannes and some here. The ones here, Jean-Claude and I can keep an eye on!'

'He never expects you to work 24/7?'

'Not expects, no . . . but we do. He's a good boss. Generous. Understanding if we have problems, like the time Jean-Claude's sister had a meningitis scare. He put the plane at our disposal so we could get to Paris quickly.'

'All this jetting about,' Carrie said, 'it's all a bit of a whirlwind to me.'

'You get used to it.'

Genifer looked at her watch, and her brow furrowed.

'I'll help with lunch,' Carrie said. 'I'm not the world's greatest cook, but I can wash lettuce and load a dishwasher!'

'Oh, it's not lunch I'm worried about,' Genifer said, checking her watch again. 'Nicos should be back by now.'

'Nicos?'

'The guy who's skippering the yacht with Carter Mills and his friends.'

'Carter Mills? The film star?'

'Yes, him. Look, sorry, I'm going to have to cut short the guided tour. I'll have to get Jean-Claude to run over to the office and see if he can get hold of Nicos on the ship-to-shore radio.'

Genifer was already halfway to the door, so Carrie turned and followed her. Hmm, she mused, it might be a great place to live with all the sunshine and glamorous people, and designer this and that at every turn, but what sort of a life was it if Genifer couldn't do something as simple as arranging lunch for friends without having to think about her job?

'Carrie, I'm sorry,' Morgan said. 'But I'm going to have to stay here.'

'I guessed as much,' Carrie said.

She carried on folding her clothes neatly, ready to pack. She was not looking forward to flying back alone one little bit. But fly back she must because tomorrow the contractor would be at Oakenbury Hall to sort the electrics before she could complete the work on the master bedroom. And she still had the nursery plan to get down on paper rather than flying around in her head as it was now. The nursery — Carrie struggled to put all thoughts about Morgan having babies with someone that wasn't her, out of her mind. She wondered if he felt guilty that he had made love to her when he had another woman in his life, but Morgan's guilt wasn't Carrie's concern right now.

'Carter Mills,' Morgan said, 'might be a big-shot US film star but he's pitifully low on manners. The idiot put everyone's lives at risk with his lager-lout behaviour.'

Carrie sighed. She'd sat, alone, at Genifer's dining table while her friend, Jean-Claude and Morgan had gone into business-mode trying to locate the missing yacht. Lunch time came and went. The lasagne Genifer had made dried up. No one had an appetite for very much when the time came for the evening meal. Carrie had eaten an apple and two nectarines and felt slightly sick. But the yacht had eventually limped into harbour, with a very drunk Carter Mills — and all his friends in the same state — shouting and swearing and alerting the press to his antics. Nicos had a nasty gash on his forehead that needed a trip to hospital to fix. A crew member had had most of his clothes ripped off in a fight. And a very expensive hand-held satnav had been thrown overboard.

'I wouldn't want their lives,' Carrie said. 'It's all a bit . . . well, false.'

'False?' Morgan said.

'Well,' Carrie said, 'it seems to me people like that think that money is the answer to everything. Trash a boat — pay for the damages. Rip a bloke's clothes to shreds — buy him some new ones. Put someone in hospital, pay for his treatment.'

'I'm part of that world, Carrie,' Morgan said quietly.

'I know,' Carrie said. 'And I don't mean to be rude, but . . . '

No, she wouldn't say what was on her mind — that she didn't think she could ever be part of that world. But already she was not liking that she wouldn't be seeing Morgan for a while. It would take at least a week to sort out the damaged yacht and begin claims procedure against Carter Mills. It was all going to get very messy with the press and possibly television being involved. Carrie had overheard Genifer telling Morgan that Sky News wanted an interview and should she give one? Morgan had said no because there was no way he was going to give Carter Mills free publicity.

'But what?' Morgan said.

Carrie pressed her lips together. She should never have asked Morgan to make love to her. For him it was probably no more than just another conquest — another notch on his considerably beautiful bedpost. But for her it had been much more — she had, she realised, fallen in love.

'Tell me, Carrie,' Morgan pleaded.

'It's not because of what happened this morning, is it?'

'No.'

'Well then, you don't have to go now. You could leave very early tomorrow and still be in time for the contractors. And we could have a repeat performance starting right now.'

'No we can't. This morning, I think I was still a bit drunk.'

'And you wouldn't have made love to me if you hadn't been? Is that what you're saying?'

Carrie was amazed to see Morgan was looking genuinely hurt and upset. She wished she could take the words back but she'd said them now. Maybe it was for the best — it would stop her getting a broken heart all over again. She lifted the lid of the case and began almost throwing her things inside.

'I've got a spare case you can have,' Morgan said, and to Carrie's ears his voice had become businesslike, detached. Nothing like the gentle and loving Morgan who had whispered so deliciously in her ear only hours before. She wanted that Morgan back so badly her body ached. But she'd probably ruined her chances for all time.

'This one's fine for my needs,' Carrie said.

'You don't have to be so stubborn.'

'I'm *not* being stubborn. This old case is absolutely fine. You're giving me a case because you've probably got hundreds of the things, all in leather, and bringing me here by private jet and buying me the kaftan . . . well, it all smacks of charity.'

Her hands were shaking now as she tried to smooth the clothes down so she could shut the lid, but they refused to be smoothed.

Morgan came to stand behind her, putting his arms around her. He grasped her hands, then turned her around to face him.

'It was not an act of charity on my part when I made love to you this morning,' he said. He kissed Carrie's forehead, and then her nose. Then his mouth found the side of her neck. 'And it is not going to be an act of charity now.'

Carrie felt as though her insides were melting with longing.

'But Ed . . . '

'Ed will wait until I drive you to Cannes Mandelieu airport — it's what I pay him for.'

'But . . . '

'No more 'buts',' Morgan said, hugging her close, before lifting her gently and laying her down on the bed. 'And *this* time I confess I have pre-planned.' He took a packet of contraceptives from his chinos and waggled it at her.

'Oh . . . '

But that was the last thing Carrie said before Morgan's mouth found hers.

★　★　★

Carrie was more than busy at Oakenbury Hall over the coming week

— organising workmen, planning the nursery. Morgan rang but each time he did Carrie was somewhere else — at the paint shop, or The Attic sourcing more material — and he was forced to leave a message on his own answerphone to say he would probably be another week, possibly two. Something else had cropped up. It didn't seem, to Carrie, that any sort of return call was needed, so she didn't ring. But then another message came asking Carrie to ring back. But she'd been so busy during the day that she'd fallen asleep, fully clothed on the bed when she got in. When she'd woken, stiff and cold, at 3 a.m. she'd deemed it too late to ring him.

On the Monday of her second week back Mrs Dawkins came bursting into the drawing room with a bunch of white freesias in her hand.

'They're for you,' Mrs Dawkins said.

'From Morgan?' Carrie said.

'Who else?' Mrs Dawkins laughed, thrusting the flowers at her.

'But he's already had roses sent to my flat.'

'Then aren't you the lucky one. My husband dropped the word flowers from his lexicon the day we married. Not that I begrudge you flowers, Miss.'

Yes, Carrie thought, I am lucky. And rude. I ought to have made an effort to ring him from my flat to thank him for the roses however tired I was.

'I'll ring him and thank him tonight, Mrs Dawkins. I'd do it from here now on my mobile but there's no signal here.'

'It'll have to be the landline then, won't it?' Mrs Dawkins said, smiling broadly. 'And my guess is he'll be glad to hear your voice. Number's on the top of the pad by the phone in the hall.'

And then Mrs Dawkins skittered off, leaving Carrie alone.

She walked slowly to the phone and tapped in the number. There was just the one ringtone in her ear before the phone was answered.

'Carrie?'

'Yes. Mrs Dawkins said I could use this phone . . . '

'Of course. Of course. Any time. Carrie, I can't tell you how good it is to hear you.'

And me, you, Carrie thought.

'Thank you for the flowers,' she said instead. 'All of them. They're beautiful.'

'I look forward to giving you more — in person. And soon, I hope. Oh blast it, I'm so sorry, Carrie . . . I've got to go. Gen's ushering a client in. Text me. I can pick up when I'm free then. Okay?'

'Okay.'

'Bye.'

'Bye,' Carrie said, but Morgan had put down the phone.

Life was always going to be like this with Morgan, wasn't it? His thoughts with her as he'd proved by sending flowers, but his body somewhere else being the big businessman that he was. Hmm . . . Carrie had lots to think about.

Text messages flew back and forth — Carrie's with brief progress reports on how work was proceeding at Oakenbury Hall, and Morgan's with short and witty comments about some of his celebrity clients. Oh, and one in which he said he wanted her to come over soon to tell him what plans she had for the villa.

But neither said they missed the other. And Morgan's idea of soon seemed to be a long time coming.

And now it was another Monday morning and seven long weeks had passed since Carrie had seen Morgan. She had a key to Oakenbury Hall but she rang the bell anyway — a courtesy to Mrs Dawkins who might be alarmed if she walked in unannounced.

But there was no answer to her ring. So Carrie unlocked the door and stepped inside, sidestepping a pile of post on the mat.

She didn't mean to look, and

191

afterwards she told herself anyone would have done the same — she couldn't help but see the name and the address on the envelope.

'*Sir* Morgan Harrington?' she said, turning the top envelope over, before rapidly flipping through the others in the pile. 'He can't be.'

But the proof that he was, was in Carrie's hands. She remembered Genifer alluding to him mixing in the upper echelons of society before killing the conversation because she had already said too much. Had Morgan instructed Genifer not to tell Carrie about his title?

'Well,' she said, 'you're not the only one who can keep secrets.'

10

'Morgan!' Carrie said, later that day, his name catching in her throat so that she couldn't be sure if she had spoken it out loud or had only thought it. She hadn't known he was coming back. And now her legs seemed to have turned to the consistency of unset jelly as she took another step down the stairs. She clutched the fabric samples designated for the nursery at Oakenbury Hall to her chest, and then slid them down protectively over her stomach. A nursery that was to be for Morgan and some other woman's child, and not her own. Their own — hers and Morgan's. A nursery for someone who would be Lady Harrington — that someone, certainly not her. She regretted giving herself so easily to Morgan now — although she didn't regret the new life growing within her because all life was precious.

'The very same,' Morgan said, hurrying towards her as she reached the bottom tread. He kissed her cheeks in the French fashion. 'You look . . . how can I describe it . . . ?' He placed his hands on Carrie's shoulders and studied her. '*Well* would sum it up. I think the Scots might call it bonny.'

'And I didn't before?' Carrie said. She wriggled out from under his hold and, skirting round him, walked across the hall to place the fabric samples on the hall table.

'You know you did,' Morgan said. 'Maybe I should have said 'weller', but there's no such word. I'll dig about in my vocabulary and see if I can come up with another one.'

He came to stand beside Carrie who wasn't sure what she should do next — leave perhaps? Right now before her heart gave her away. Right now before she told Morgan she was expecting his child — she'd bought four pregnancy tests and used them on different days at different times and they had all given the same, positive, result. But the nearness of him, her desire for him, made speech impossible.

'Got it!' Morgan said. '*Blooming* — that's the word.'

Carrie closed her eyes — it was as though he had seen right through her and knew. She swallowed hard. This should be her moment, but still the words she needed to say wouldn't come.

'The drawing room is finished,' she said instead. 'Come and look.'

'Lead me,' Morgan said. 'I'll close my eyes and you can guide me in, and tell me when to open them.'

He reached for Carrie's hand.

'Don't be silly,' she said.

'Since when has holding the hand of a beautiful woman been silly?'

Before Carrie could put her hand behind her back or tuck it under an armpit, Morgan grasped it.

'I like surprises,' he said.

But possibly not the one I'm going to

do my best not to give you, Carrie thought.

'All right, then,' Carrie said. His hand felt warm and solid and protective around hers as she led him through the doorway. 'You can open them now.'

'Wow!' Morgan said. 'You've worked wonders. Clever, clever you.'

Then he spun her round and hugged her to him. She felt his lips against her hair, felt his hand glide up her back until it reached the nape of her neck. He hugged her even closer.

'You like it, then?' she said, placing her hands against his chest and pushing herself gently away from him. 'You don't mind that I've hung one of my paintings over the fireplace? It was a huge space crying out for something to fill it.'

She pointed to the study of peonies — huge blowsy blooms the size of Savoy cabbages she'd done when in the sixth form at school — and which just about filled any wall on which she hung it in her own home. Here it looked as though it belonged. Well, she thought it did.

Morgan seemed to be taking an age to respond.

'There are peonies in the garden, I noticed,' Carrie said. 'You can change it for something else if you want to. But, well, my painting makes a nice link, I think.'

'It does indeed. Add it to the cost.'

'No. It's a gift. If you like it. It's too big for my flat, but it will . . . '

' . . . do in here?'

Now who was putting words in other people's mouths as Morgan had accused her of doing a few times. Carrie bit her lip. This wasn't going how she had planned it to go.

Morgan threw a mock-sad face — echoing her own expression no doubt.

'Cheer up, Carrie. The painting's fabulous, and you know it. It enhances this room, gives it warmth. In fact, it makes the place look so wonderful I'm almost tempted to change my mind and make this my main home.'

'Only almost?' Carrie said.

'I think so. Even though sorting out the Carter Mills mess was the downside of what I do and took far, far, longer than I expected it to, it's taught me one thing — I should be on the spot 24/7.'

'Oh,' Carrie said.

'That was a very loaded 'oh'?'

'It wasn't meant to be,' Carrie said. She struggled for what to say next, but it seemed being newly pregnant had robbed her of cohesive thought much of the time. 'But, but ... I thought Jean-Claude seemed on top of the game. And Genifer.'

'They're both great. But they want a family sometime, and they won't be able to give a family and me 24/7. I couldn't ask that of them.'

'But it would be okay to leave your own family to work?' Carrie clapped a hand to her mouth. 'I'm sorry. I shouldn't have said that.'

'No, perhaps you shouldn't,' Morgan said.

He walked slowly around the room, touching a cushion here, a newly upholstered chair there. He strolled languidly towards the window and pulled the drapes closed, before opening them again. Then he turned to face Carrie.

'But we all say things we shouldn't sometimes, so you're forgiven.' Morgan's smile was wide — the smile reaching his eyes. 'Now, am I right in thinking the master bedroom is also completed?'

'You are,' Carrie said, her heart unsteady in her breast, as she felt herself drowning in the strength of his smile. 'But you know where it is. Go on up.'

'Not on my own. You're coming.'

'I, I, I . . . can't,' Carrie stuttered. 'I haven't got time. I've got to price up another job on my way home.'

'Carrie, what's wrong?' Morgan strode across the room towards her. 'I thought you'd be pleased to see me? You must have only just arrived because it's not even 9.30 a.m. yet, for heaven's sake!'

'You didn't tell me you'd be here today.'

'I don't have to make an appointment to turn up at my own house, Carrie,' Morgan said.

'Well, I know *that*!' Carrie said.

Morgan wrinkled his forehead in puzzlement.

'This sounds dangerously like we're having an argument. Shall I go out and ring you on my mobile to let you know I'm here, and come back in again?'

'No, of course not. It's just that you surprised me, that's all.' Carrie pulled herself mentally together. She was a professional for goodness' sake, doing a job, and this man was her boss. 'I'll show you the master bedroom now, shall I?'

'I can hardly wait!'

And that, Carrie thought, as she led the way up the stairs, conscious of Morgan's eyes on her and the wobbliness of her legs, is what I'm afraid of.

'This . . . ' Morgan said, the second

he threw wide the master bedroom door and stepped inside, 'is wonderful.'

'I'm glad you like it.'

'And you've kept the old Persian rug. You could have bought new.'

'New?' Carrie said. She walked over to stand on the rug, and ran the point of her toe over a section of the design. 'But this is *perfect* in this room. Look!' she carried on, waving her arms around like some sort of demented windmill, afraid Morgan was now going to find fault where she, herself, could see none — this was the best bit of interior design she'd ever done, 'I've picked out that wonderful faded lavender shade for the walls. And I darkened it slightly for the paint on the picture rails.'

Morgan turned full circle in the room, drinking it all in with his eyes.

'So you have. I'm impressed.'

'And I didn't see the point in spending money where money didn't need to be spent. Not that, you know, I'm telling you how to spend your own money or anything.'

She was turning into a gibbering idiot now, wasn't she — she'd come over all self-defensive when she didn't have to be.

'I like a woman capable of making an executive decision,' Morgan said, smiling warmly at her. 'That rug's over a hundred and fifty years old. I remember playing on it as a small boy. Thank you, Carrie for bringing that memory back for me. And for making such a good job of this room.'

'Not too girlie?'

'Definitely not.'

'Good. You did say to make it the sort of room I would want to sleep in.'

'And do you?'

'It was a hypothetical request at the time,' Carrie said. 'Oh, and I've taken the liberty of buying a new mattress. The other one was like a board.'

'Good idea.' He walked to the bed and sat on the edge. 'I don't like the idea of you sleeping on a board.'

Carrie gulped — with him, did he mean?

'Come and sit down, Carrie.'

'I've already tested it, thank you,' she said, walking in the opposite direction from the bed towards the window and folding her arms across her chest, staring out over the garden.

'You think of everything,' Morgan said, standing up — and his voice was rather clipped, Carrie thought. 'Can you show me your plans for the nursery now?'

He strode towards the door.

* * *

'What name shall I make the invoice out to?' Carrie said.

She'd shown Morgan the mood board for the nursery but he hadn't expressed the interest in it she'd expected him to. And now they were sitting opposite one another at the kitchen table, a fresh cafétière of coffee between them and a pile of toast she'd made for Morgan. Carrie had been buttering it before she realised he hadn't asked her to make it — for some reason she'd simply gone and done it. Wanted to do it.

'*My* name. Who else's?'

'I mean Morgan Harrington, or *Sir* Morgan Harrington?'

She heard the sharp intake of Morgan's breath at the question.

'Who told you about my title?' His eyes darkened as he spoke. He looked angry. 'Was it Genifer?'

'No!'

'Mrs Dawkins then?'

'Not her either.'

'Then who?'

'No one. I arrived early one morning and picked up your post off the mat.'

'That's Mrs Dawkins' job. It's what I pay her for, for goodness' sake.'

'Well, she wasn't here. She had a tummy bug that day, actually. So, I did what any normal person would do and picked it up and put it on the hall table. I couldn't help noticing.'

Carrie felt irritated with herself that she was explaining her actions to

Morgan, but there was also the aspect that she needed to stand up for herself.

'Why didn't you tell me?'

'Would it have made any difference if I had?'

'I don't know.'

'Oh yes, you do,' Morgan said. 'I knew there was a change in how you thought of me the second I walked in the door earlier. There was a massive shift in our relationship. The girl who'd offered herself to me so warmly, so lovingly, so willingly . . . '

'I shouldn't have done that. It's not how I normally behave.'

'I'm pleased to hear it. But please let me finish. The girl you were then had been replaced by an ice-maiden. My previous experience with women has been exactly the opposite. Once a woman knows I'm titled, they can't wait to get into my bed, get the ring on their finger, get those four little letters in front of their name.'

'I've already got four letters in front of mine — MISS,' Carrie said.

Morgan groaned and put his head in his hands.

Carrie left him to his thoughts. She began to cut a slice of toast into fingers simply for something to do. There was something troubling Morgan deeply but she would wait for him to tell her.

'I wasn't the heir,' he said, taking his hands from his face. 'Talbot was. I made a point of not telling Georgina my family history. And I kept her apart from Talbot and my father as long as I could. Genifer and Jean-Claude, of course, honoured their promise not to give my personal details to anyone. But she was pushing for an engagement and I did love her — then. Or thought I did . . . '

Morgan's voice trailed away again as though it was painful remembering, never mind saying the words. Carrie offered him a piece of toast which he took and chewed slowly.

'So, once the ring was on her finger I had to introduce her to my family. The day she realised Talbot was the heir and she could be Lady Harrington if she married him and not me, was the day she . . . '

'Changed sides?'

'That's one way of putting it.' Morgan took a long slug of coffee. 'I should have learned from that, but I didn't.'

'In what way?'

'I'd like a £50 note for every woman who's told me she was carrying my child expecting me to suggest instant marriage, only to decide they weren't actually pregnant in the first place when I declined to do so.'

Morgan almost spat the words out.

'Because they wanted a title?' Carrie's voice was a whisper. How could she tell him about the baby now?

'Wouldn't you?'

'No,' Carrie said. 'For one thing this is the twenty-first century we are living in and women can bring up children on their own. And secondly, I think it's a dirty trick to lie like that. But presumably you have someone in mind who doesn't sink to such base behaviour to get her hands on a title if you've asked me to prepare all this?'

She swept an arm across the mood board and the fabric samples she'd laid out on the table to show Morgan.

'I have. But I'm not sure she feels the same way about me now. Which is a bit of a shame because I thought — knew actually — she might be the one. I thought I was a step closer to meeting my father's wishes.'

'You would go ahead and marry someone just so you can provide an heir, carry on the family name?'

Carrie knew her voice had risen at least an octave; one minute she'd been feeling so sorry for Morgan and the next she was outraged at his words.

'Don't put words in my mouth, Carrie, please.' Morgan re-filled his mug with coffee then did the same for Carrie and slid her mug back across the table towards her. 'Our coffee's going cold.'

Carrie picked up the drink and held

it to her mouth, but she was overcome by a wave of nausea. That had been happening a lot recently with certain food and drinks. But she needed to drink something because her mouth had gone dry with nerves. She sipped on the liquid cautiously, but it tasted bitter.

'I think I'm going to have to go home,' she said. 'I feel like I'm going down with something.'

A something that's going to turn into about seven pounds of baby — an heir, or heiress, to Oakenbury Hall and an awful lot more in the south of France. Did she have the right to deny her child that? She couldn't begin to ponder that now — she just had to get out of this kitchen and her nearness to Morgan.

She stood up and pushed back her chair, the legs scraping on the tiled floor. She put her hands over her ears because the sound was so loud — and that was another thing since her body had changed . . . sounds were louder, smells more pungent.

But as she turned to go a jolt of dizziness made her grab for the chair back, but she missed and stumbled. Morgan raced to her side.

'Carrie, what's wrong?'

Morgan put one arm around Carrie's back and placed his free hand under her elbow. Carrie knew she should insist on going home, but she felt terrible. Unnerved by Morgan's return, yes, but her mind was in turmoil about her future too.

'Perhaps if I rest on the couch for a while I'll be fine again soon.'

'For as long as you like,' Morgan said.

And he led her into the drawing room and helped her onto the couch, and Carrie let herself be led. It felt so good to be looked after if only for a little while.

Before she left she'd have to tell Morgan she wouldn't be accepting his commission to re-design his villa at La Bocca, wouldn't she? Because if she did he'd soon find out about the baby. And there was no way she was going to let him think she was tricking him into marriage.

As soon as she felt less dizzy and less sick, she'd drive home.

11

'What?'

It couldn't be — Morgan must have made a mistake. Carrie had the cheque he'd given her but there was an extra nought on the amount to what she'd written on her invoice.

Damn, she was going to have to ring him and tell him, wasn't she? She grabbed her phone from the table and scrolled down to Morgan's number.

'Carrie!' Morgan said, not giving her a chance to speak when he answered her call. 'How are you? There's nothing wrong is there?'

'Um, well . . . '

'Make my day — tell me you've changed your mind about taking on the job at my villa.'

'No, it's not that.'

'But it's something?'

'Yes. You've made a mistake with the

amount on the cheque you gave me.'

'No mistake,' Morgan said cheerily.

'Well, I can't accept it.'

'Reasons — at least three. Starting . . . now!'

'Stop it, Morgan. It's not funny. I need . . . '

' . . . the money? There you are then, accept my cheque. Pay it in, pay for your mother's conservatory, buy a new car. Get some new clothes.'

'What's wrong with my clothes?'

'Nothing wrong with your clothes exactly . . . ' he began, but Carrie stopped him.

★   ★   ★

'Could you put a cheque for the correct amount in the post, and I'll tear this one up?'

'No. I want you to have the money.'

'But not this much,' Carrie said.

She ripped the cheque into tiny squares.

'Was that the sound of what I think it was?'

213

'Yes. Your cheque is now confetti.'

'You didn't have to do that,' Morgan said.

'Yes, I did.'

'I'll just have to write another then, won't I?'

And then Morgan killed the call.

* * *

'I don't want a drink, thank you,' Carrie said as Morgan stepped into her hallway clutching a bottle of champagne to his oh-so-sexy chest, and looking impossibly handsome and desirable, and kissable.

'I haven't offered you one yet.'

Morgan tilted his head on one side and smiled at Carrie.

'I know, but look what happened last time.'

Instinctively, Carrie placed a hand on her stomach, and then quickly took it away again in case Morgan noticed and was that rare thing for a man — intuitive — and began asking awkward questions.

'I thought what happened last time was rather lovely.'

And so do I in my heart of hearts, Carrie thought. Oh God, no — she was coming over all teary again. It must be the hormones. She'd been feeling rather weepy lately, and now she didn't trust herself to speak in case those tears fell, so she simply shrugged.

'The number of zeros doesn't mean much to me, Carrie. I'd consider it money well spent.'

'For sex?' Carrie yelled — goodness, she'd found her voice then, and suddenly her tears seemed to have turned to ice. If Morgan Harrington thought this was a pay-off for sex . . . well, he had another think coming.

'For services rendered then?'

'Isn't that what . . . '

No, Carrie couldn't say it, even if she was thinking it.

'You, little lady,' Morgan said, pushing the door shut behind him, and taking Carrie's hand, 'are a class act at putting words in my mouth. Words I would never use about a lady.'

'I'm not your lady!' Carrie said, her hand snug in Morgan's as he walked towards her sitting room.

'Well, we'll have to see if we can change that, won't we?' Morgan said.

He leaned towards Carrie as though to kiss her. But she jumped back.

'I don't think so,' Carrie said, disentangling her hand from Morgan's. 'You told me yourself that after Georgina . . . '

'Georgina is history. And I've been doing a lot of thinking lately.'

'As in thinking about finding someone to have your baby to honour your father's wishes?'

Carrie knew it was a spiteful thing to say, but she couldn't help herself. Common sense told her that the further she pushed him away from her emotionally the better it would be, although her heart was saying differently.

'Heir is the word you're looking for, Carrie.'

'But what if it's an heiress?'

'Then we'd just have to try again, wouldn't we?'

We? Did he really mean her and him? And what would his reaction be if she told him right now that she was pregnant with his child? She had a feeling she would see his onyx eyes darken, bore into her, hate her for trying to trap him — before walking out and slamming the door behind him. Having a baby together should always be a joint decision, to Carrie's mind.

'But not with someone who tries to trick you into marriage?' she said quietly.

'Definitely not,' Morgan said. 'Most definitely *not*.'

And that was precisely the answer I expected, Carrie thought — she'd have been a fool to imagine he'd think otherwise.

⋆ ⋆ ⋆

'You what?' Carrie said. She couldn't believe what she was hearing.

The contractor on the end of the line was saying he was pulling out of the job at Oakenbury Hall. Something bigger had come up, and she could sue him through the small courts if she wanted to, but he wasn't bothered. The job he had now would more than pay her costs.

'You heard, sweetheart,' the man said.

'I'm not your sweetheart!'

Honestly! He just didn't give a damn about letting her down, did he?

'Glad to hear it with a temper on you like that,' the man said. 'Now I'll leave you to get on and find someone else . . . '

But Carrie didn't hear any more as she slammed down the phone. She began to rifle through her list of contractors but no one could fit her in at such short notice. She tried the Yellow Pages, but with the same result. No decorator worth his salt would be free to start a job the same day of asking, she knew that — anyone really good would be booked up months in advance.

There was nothing for it. She'd just have to start the work on the nursery at Oakenbury Hall herself, wouldn't she? And the irony of it wasn't lost on her either.

⋆   ⋆   ⋆

Much to Carrie's amazement, she began to feel at peace — a sense of calmness — as she worked. Instead of rushing the work through as she'd thought she might, she worked slowly — each brushstroke perfect, each piece of wallpaper she hung smoothed of bubbles at the first attempt.

She arrived before nine each morning, and left after six in the evening and yet she wasn't tired. It was as though something — or someone — was watching over her.

And now the nursery was almost finished. The soft-furnishing company had arrived that morning with the drapes for the windows and — at Carrie's request — with an extra three yards of the same material so that she could make cushion covers. She was looking forward to recovering the large, feather-filled, cushions she'd found in the room. She imagined a small child curling up on them, cuddling a soft toy in sleep, or maybe looking at a picture book.

The single bed that Morgan had agreed she could buy had been placed against the wall, but as yet no cot had been ordered. At what stage should she think about buying a cot for her own baby she wondered? Or maybe a crib to begin with — something small. Mrs Dawkins had said there was a crib up in the attic somewhere and that she'd ask Morgan to bring it down when he returned. Although when Morgan was going to return from Cannes to look for the crib, Carrie had no idea — already the two weeks he'd said he'd be away had turned into four.

And her body was changing shape

with her growing baby. Thank goodness the fashion for summer was loose smocks, lots of fabric, copious gathers.

The evenings were getting lighter and longer. And now, the paintwork on the three guest bedrooms had been sanded down, and the walls prepared ready for papering, Carrie was reluctant to return to her flat.

'Ah, there you are,' Carrie said, coming into the kitchen. Mrs Dawkins was folding her overall, ready to put in the pantry until she needed it in the morning. 'I'm glad I've caught you before you left.'

'Only just,' Mrs Dawkins said. 'Is there something you need?'

'Not really . . . well . . . '

'What is it, dear?'

Mrs Dawkins laid a hand on Carrie's arm.

Carrie shrugged, and Mrs Dawkins took her hand away again.

'You're not doing too much, are you?' she said.

'No, I'm fine, thanks. Everything's

going well at the moment. In fact I think I'm ahead of schedule.'

'So, what did you want me for?' Mrs Dawkins grabbed her bag and began scrabbling in it, her fingers finding a bunch of keys. 'Only I need to be off now.'

'Yes, of course,' Carrie said. Her mind struggled to come up with something to say. She couldn't say, I don't want to go home, I want to feel near to Morgan.

'Anything else?' Mrs Dawkins asked.

'Yes, there is something,' she said. 'Do you think Morgan would mind if I stop on for a while? I haven't got a garden at my flat, you see, and I'd like to sit outside and make a start on the cushion covers.'

'Of course he won't, dear. He won't mind at all.' Mrs Dawkins snapped her bag shut, shrugged on her jacket and walked towards the back door. 'See you tomorrow. Oh,' she added, patting her own stomach. 'And what you're doing is called 'nesting' in these parts.'

And then she was gone.

Nesting? Is that what I'm doing? And Mrs Dawkins knew why, didn't she? She'd have to tell Morgan now before someone else did.

But first she'd go out into the garden and watch the sunset.

12

And that was where Morgan found her. She leapt to her feet with surprise when she saw him. A breeze blew her top around her, accentuating her now very obvious baby bump.

She heard him breathe in deeply, letting it all out slowly.

Then he said, 'You're expecting a baby?'

'I am.'

'Really?'

'Really,' Carrie said, running her hands down over her bump.

'Dare I ask?'

'Yes. Yours. We locked the stable door after the horse had bolted in the birth control department, didn't we?'

'We did rather, didn't we? Oh, Carrie . . . I . . . '

'And, just so we're clear, I don't want a penny from you.'

Carrie started to walk towards the house, but Morgan soon caught up with her because she was shaking so much and her legs were barely supporting her.

'You can't go anywhere in that state,' Morgan said, laying a hand oh-so-gently on her shoulder and all Carrie wanted to do was lean in to him, but she shrugged him off.

'This state is going to be with me for a good many months yet,' Carrie said.

'So, we'll have plenty of time to talk about it,' Morgan said, holding wide the back door for Carrie. 'I'll make us some tea. Unless you're off tea?'

'I was for a couple of weeks,' Carrie said, touched that he'd thought to ask. 'And off a lot of other things too, but that seems to have passed, thank goodness.'

'Good,' Morgan said. He set about tea-making, humming a snatch of something to himself. 'Biscuit with the tea, now you're eating for two?' he asked, handing Carrie her mug.

'Or three,' Carrie said.

'You're not?' Morgan said.

Carrie gave a little 'who knows' shrug, and Morgan grinned as though the thought of sudden multi-parenthood might not be so bad an idea.

'Well, Caroline Fraser, you have surprised me.'

'I'm not Caroline.'

'Just Carrie?'

'Not that either.'

Morgan raised a quizzical eyebrow.

'What other possibilities are there?' he asked.

'Carenza,' Carrie said with a groan. 'Awful isn't it?'

'No,' Morgan said. 'I think it's rather wonderful. Carenza.'

He drew out the name so that to Carrie's ears it sounded like a warm caress. Coming from his lips it didn't sound so bad at all — in fact it sounded rather wonderful, as Morgan himself had said.

'Am I the last to know about the baby?' Morgan asked.

'The first. After me obviously. I

haven't even told Mum yet because she's always out somewhere with Paul these days and over the phone doesn't seem the way to tell a mother something like that.'

'Indeed not,' Morgan said.

Carrie sipped her tea, glad of its warming comfort. She ought to be going soon but there was so much she and Morgan needed to talk about.

'I've drawn up the plans for the last two bedrooms — the smaller ones,' Carrie said, just for something to say, something to keep her at Oakenbury Hall. 'And I've prepared the walls and paintwork, sorted the mood boards.'

'I don't want you overworking.'

'I might be pregnant but I haven't lost all common sense,' Carrie said. 'I'll know when to stop. Right now I feel fine, so if it's all right with you I'll be here most days. How long are you staying anyway?'

'That all depends on your answer to my next question.'

'Which is?' Carrie said.

'Carenza, will you marry me? Will you be my lady?'

Carrie gulped. She hadn't been expecting that.

Morgan reached for Carrie's hand. He lifted it to his lips, and Carrie felt the tingle fizzle through her body. All her instincts told her she wanted to be with this man forever. But should she be even considering saying yes to his question? Could she go through the process of organising a wedding again? Might Morgan change his mind at the last moment as Aaron had? And, more importantly, was he only marrying her because she was pregnant?

'Not at the moment, Morgan, no,' Carrie said. 'Because I'm not sure about your reasons for asking me.'

★ ★ ★

'Gen?' Carrie said, the second her friend's excited voice trilled in her ear.

'Right first time,' Genifer said. 'But I guess you've been expecting my call.'

'Um, no,' Carrie said, 'but it's great to hear you.'

She had a feeling Morgan had something to do with the call, but no way was she going to ask — she'd wait for Genifer to reveal the reason.

'Oh, well, I expect Morgan forgot to tell you. But it's a yes to his invitation.'

'To?' Carrie said.

'To come over and see what you've done to Oakenbury Hall! Honestly, Carrie, you should have heard the way he was singing your praises! There's going to be a dinner party! The Saturday after next! Don't say you didn't know.'

But that was only ten days away — when had Morgan thought he was going to tell her, give her a chance to finish everything off to the sort of standard required to accept the first guests in the refurbished rooms?

Even though Morgan asked her to marry him every single day now, she hadn't said yes yet. And despite his pleadings for her to stop the night she always went home when her day's work was done.

'Well, I've been busy. We both have. I expect he meant to tell me but forgot.'

'He said you'd say that,' Genifer said with a giggle. 'And that's not all!'

'Spill the beans,' Carrie said.

'He's only gone and given Jean-Claude and me joint managing director roles! We're going to be running things exclusively over here! Isn't that great? If the family we want comes along, then we'll rethink my role in things. But hey! As I said — great!'

'Great,' Carrie said.

'You don't sound like you think it's great one little bit! You sound a bit peeved, if I may say so.'

'I'm not. I'm just surprised. Morgan told me he couldn't make Oakenbury Hall his main home, and not so long ago either.'

'Well, obviously, he's changed his mind for some reason. Not entirely a female prerogative, changing one's mind.'

'Obviously not,' Carrie said.

'So, all you've got to do now is find something wonderful to wear, isn't it?'

'I suppose so,' Carrie said.

'And no charity shop bargains, Carrie!' Genifer said, laughing. 'Something that Cinderella might wear to the ball — after her transformation by magic wand, obviously, not the rags she went in.'

And then Genifer made kissy noises down the line and was gone.

★　★　★

It was the day of the dinner party — Genifer and Jean-Claude were due to arrive soon. And Louise. Carrie had at last finished the guest rooms and was pleased with her work. She was rearranging the cushions on a chaise longue one last time when she heard Morgan open the door.

'Remember you said you couldn't face organising a wedding again?' he said, coming to stand beside her.

'Yes,' Carrie said warily.

'Well, you don't have to if you don't want to. Because I have. Just us, you and me, and two witnesses the vicar will provide. But you can change any or all of those arrangements.'

'No,' Carrie said. She reached for his hands and held them tightly.

'You won't marry me?'

'No. Yes. No. Oh, what I mean is, I don't want to thing a change. I like as things . . .'

Oh God, she was talking gobbledygook again.

Morgan kissed the tip of her nose.

'The second I saw you standing on my doorstep,' Morgan said, 'and the second you opened your mouth and got your words all muddled up, I fell in love with you.'

'And I you,' Carrie said. She leaned towards Morgan and kissed his lips — just a gentle kiss that didn't linger but it would tell him everything about how she felt. 'And I'm still muddling my words up!'

'So, was that a no you don't want to marry me, or . . . '

'It was no, I don't want you to change a thing about the arrangements. They sound perfect to me.'

★   ★   ★

'This is *your* church?' Carrie asked, as Morgan led her around the edge of his lake.

Carrie was wearing a cornflower-blue ankle-length dress that billowed around her legs in the slight breeze. It had spaghetti straps with tiny silver butter-flies embroidered on them, and a v-shaped neckline. Simple and elegant.

On her head she was wearing a circlet of tiny white flowers picked from one of the shrubs in the garden that Morgan had told her was called 'Bridal wreath'. Her shoes were ballet pumps in the same shade of blue as her dress, and her bouquet flowers, now dangling from her free hand, a fistful of sweet peas grown by Mrs Dawkins' husband, Ken, and picked that morning and tied with raffia.

'Chapel. It goes with the house. I've always kept the licence for marriages up to date.'

'Just as well,' Carrie laughed.

She couldn't quite believe that in half an hour's time she'd be a married woman; Lady Harrington. She said the name over and over to herself in her head and still it seemed strange, alien almost. But she was going to have to get used to it — wanted to get used to it.

'I wonder what they'll all say when we turn up for the dinner party as man and wife?' Morgan asked.

'Oh, we'll be bombarded with questions, I should think. And there'll be an element of shock because they think they've only been invited for a dinner party, not a wedding breakfast,' Carrie said.

'Happy for us though, I hope.'

'I almost told my mother. She's going to be cross she's not witnessing my marriage.'

'Louise will be fine about it, trust me.'

'I will,' Carrie said.

Morgan laughed. 'Just remember to say those two little words when the vicar asks!'

For answer, Carrie stretched towards him and kissed his cheek.

'But you can still pull out if you want to. You don't have to marry me just because of the baby.'

'Oh, Carrie,' Morgan said, stopping to fold her in his arms and hug her tight. 'How can you ever think I'd want to? Even before I found my father's letter and read about his wish for me to have children, I'd already fallen in love with you. I actually saw and heard our children in my head more than a few times.'

'So did I!' Carrie said. 'But I never for a minute thought you'd feel the same.'

'But I've proved you wrong,' Morgan said, smiling down at her. 'From that moment the idea was firmly planted in my mind to make a nursery.'

'And I thought you were doing it for someone else.'

'I was afraid to make my feelings known too soon . . . you know.'

'Past histories?' Carrie said. 'Georgina and Talbot were yours, and Aaron was mine.'

'Time to leave them behind?' Morgan said as they reached the open double doors of the chapel.

'Definitely,' Carrie said, gripping tightly to Morgan's hand.

And, head held high, with joy filling her heart like tiny fireworks going off, spreading warmth and light through her body, Carrie walked with Morgan down the slate floor of the chapel that was decorated with wonderfully scented lemon roses on the pew ends, to become his lady.

We do hope that you have enjoyed reading this large print book.

Did you know that all of our titles are available for purchase?

We publish a wide range of high quality large print books including:
Romances, Mysteries, Classics
General Fiction
Non Fiction and Westerns

Special interest titles available in large print are:
The Little Oxford Dictionary
Music Book, Song Book
Hymn Book, Service Book

Also available from us courtesy of Oxford University Press:
Young Readers' Dictionary
(large print edition)
Young Readers' Thesaurus
(large print edition)

For further information or a free brochure, please contact us at:
Ulverscroft Large Print Books Ltd.,
The Green, Bradgate Road, Anstey,
Leicester, LE7 7FU, England.
Tel: (00 44) **0116 236 4325**
Fax: (00 44) **0116 234 0205**

AN UNUSUAL INHERITANCE

Jean M. Long

Eliza Ellis has a lot on her plate. Although she teaches part-time at the local school, her passion is for baking and cake decoration. When she inherits Lilac Cottage, much to everyone's surprise, she decides to move in rather than sell up. But she also inherits a sitting tenant, in the form of Greg Holt . . . When Eliza gets involved in a new baking enterprise in the village, old memories are stirred up — and Greg knows more than he is telling . . .